A WINE RED SILENCE

A WINE RED SILENCE

GEORGE L. DUNCAN

CAPSTONE FICTION

WATERFORD, VIRGINIA

A Wine Red Silence

Published in the U.S. by:
Capstone Publishing Group LLC
P.O. Box 8
Waterford, VA 20197

Visit Capstone Fiction at
www.capstonefiction.com

Cover design by David LaPlaca/debest design co.

ISBN: 978-1-60290-137-7

To Amy, Dave, Dan, Gene and Misty:
writing group members who read
some of the chapters...and liked them.

To two members of a long-ago writing group:
Geoff—a good friend who left us much too soon.
Shelly—who now has a medical degree and will,
hopefully,
be with us for a long, long time.

And to Ann:
a courageous lady
and one of the Lord's better creations.

One

I got the first piece of bad news when Mullet claimed there was a contract out on my life. He then promised to give additional details. For five hundred dollars.

We were sitting at an outside table of the Driftwood restaurant, an upscale establishment where the tables are expertly fashioned to reflect the name. Sunlight reflected off our tall glasses. Twenty yards from us waves lapped at the shore. Mullet grabbed the lifeguard tower filled with pepper and shook it over his scrambled eggs. Nervousness and a beach breeze affected his aim. A few black flecks flew across his plate and onto the blue tablecloth.

Words spurt from Mullet like water from a hydrant when he's agitated. "Only five hundred, Jerry. You can't turn down a deal like that. How much is your life worth?"

"Last time I checked, only about two-fifty on the open market."

"You underestimate yourself, Jerry. A genrich man like you. You have all those high-quality genes. They gotta be worth more than that." Mullet chewed and swallowed the scrambled eggs, then washed them down with a swig of his beer.

Mullet likes beer for breakfast, and for lunch and dinner. When he talks, he likes to gesticulate. He's got curly black hair. A mustache. Dark eyes.

He raised his hand but pointed his fingers back at his chest. "Jerry, I might be putting myself in danger. It's because I like you that I've taking this risk."

"And for five hundred dollars."

"A man has to make a living. If I uncover information that others find worthwhile, I figure they owe me. Times are tough. I could ask a lot more, but because we're friends I'm giving you a break."

I smiled. Mullet has been prowling the beaches—and various minor criminal enterprises—of northeast Florida for almost 20 years. He does pick up random bits of information. What he lacks in honesty, he makes up for in zeal.

"Jerry, would I lie to you?"

"Yes," I told him. "And you often have."

"OK, but not about this. This is serious. Buddy, from time to time you have helped me out. I don't want to see anything happen to you. But a man..."

"Has to make a living," I said, finishing the sentence for him. I reached in my wallet. I had stopped at an ATM on the way. Since Mullet had asked for the meeting, I figured money would be involved. I counted out three bills and laid them on the table.

"Two hundred and fifty, Mullet. If your story is credible, you get the rest."

His hands swept up the bills and tucked them firmly in his pocket.

"So why would anyone want me killed?"

"Revenge. Rumor is you killed Wes Meeks."

"What?"

He shrugged. "Just repeating the rumor. Old man Merrill wants revenge on the Liquidator who cemeteried his son."

"I had nothing to do with that."

"The whispers are you did, Jerry."

I didn't know whether to be indignant, angry, or stunned. I settled for a mixture of all three. "The whispers are wrong. Meeks was killed a week ago. I just got back in the city

Monday. I've been out of state. Besides, I'm no Liquidator."

"Hey, I believe you, Jerry. Meeks won't. The old man's rich but not quite right in the head. Maybe that's why the son turned out to be a psycho, although he was supposedly genrich like you. Wes Meeks was in the killzone and somebody got him."

"You leave town for a week and..."

"Perhaps you'd better leave again, but not before you give me the other two hundred and fifty. The older Meeks has bananas for brains, but he's ruthless. What's after you may not be human."

I frowned. "A robot?"

"A special one." Mullet tapped his head with a finger. "It's not just software, Jerry. An intelligent killer. A Jackal."

I shook my head. "No one has created artificial intelligence yet. No one has perfected a Jackal."

Mullet shrugged. "Maybe they have. One is aimed at you. A thing that doesn't need to eat, sleep, or worry about consequences. What are they going to do when they find him? Turn him off?"

"I thought this was going to be just another routine day."

"The thing could be anywhere. It might be like a Courier. Flesh-colored. Can't distinguish them from humans." He looked around the restaurant, shifting a nervous gaze from one spot to another. "By the way, could I get the rest of the money now?"

"Your concern for my welfare is touching."

I reached in my wallet and took out more bills. When he reached for them, I pulled my hand back. "You know my name isn't really Jerry."

"Jerico, Jerico," Mullet said, as he grabbed the money. He shot another furtive look at the door, then turned his gaze back on me.

"Out of town? Really?"

"Yes."

"Well, it makes sense, Jerry."

"What makes sense?"

"Pointing the finger at you. A Liquidator waits until you're out of town. He knows Meeks will want revenge. He starts a rumor or makes sure something ties you to the crime. Then he walks free."

I nodded. "Plausible. But Liquidators don't incriminate other people in their...activities."

"This one did."

A waiter brought the bill. I placed two twenties in the black rectangular tray. "And Mullet, when he brings back the change, leave a tip."

"Me Jerry? Me buddy?"

"Yes, you."

My streak of bad luck continued after I drove to my office and parked. A half dozen steps away from the car, the Skulls ambushed me. Two pairs of steel-strong dark arms threw me against the parking garage wall, then frisked me for weapons, the metallic hands poking into my ribs and back. Skullcrushers got their nickname the old-fashioned way—and they've earned it. One grabbed my arms while the other landed a hard punch to my abdomen. I gasped for air.

Skulls are strong but lightweight. If they have some wear and tear on them, or are shoddily built, the best defense is to toss them against a wall and hope something breaks loose. If you get the chance, that is.

The second jackhammer punch spun my head around. My vision blurred. The dark shades bobbed and weaved in tune to the throbbing pain in my head. They shoved me into a car and barked an order to the autocomputer. In a couple of minutes the car stopped. The Skulls hauled me roughly through a second parking garage and bounced me off an elevator wall. As the doors closed I slid down on the floor. The jolt cleared my vision but increased the pounding between the temples. My gaze stayed on the two dark figures.

"Like the color. Who's your fashion coordinator?"

Manufacturers never get fancy with Skullcrusher design. Black alloy. Red sensors for eyes. They stayed silent. Not a great deal of verbal software. Of course, there's not much consumer demand for articulate and erudite Skullcrushers.

When the elevator stopped, the two picked me up and walked me down the hall. They opened one door and tossed me in. I saw enough to be surprised. The building was the Volusia County Courthouse annex, and this section belonged to the state attorney.

Interrogation rooms are sparse. I sat in the one wooden chair before the secondhand desk. My two dark companions stood silently at the back of the room. A narrow stream of blood flowed from the corner of my mouth, and I dabbed at it with a handkerchief. I didn't look forward to the next few days. When I get punched in the mouth, I get mouth ulcers. Clumps of them. Which makes it difficult to eat or talk. It's something writers leave out in all the private detective manuals. For all our medical high-tech advances, we have not yet conquered the mouth ulcer.

The door opened, and Assistant State Attorney Benjamin Adonal walked in, a grim look on his stony, pale face. As usual, he was dressed impeccably. Gray suit, gray shirt and slacks, but a blue tie indicated an early morning wild and crazy mood. He leaned against the desk and crossed his arms.

"Good morning, Jerico."

I managed a crooked smile. "It's morning, but 'good' is a matter of opinion. Right now, mine is running negative." I yanked my thumb toward the back of the room. "By the way, your friends violated about fifteen of my Constitutional rights."

He yawned and scratched his jaw. "Well, the courts aren't as picky nowadays as they were some years ago."

"When did you guys start using Skullcrushers? You do have Trackers. Or, as a last resort, you could have called my office."

"Budgets. A good Tracker costs close to twenty thousand. They have to be top-of-the-line, grade-A robots. Whereas confiscated Skullcrushers can be modified cheaply."

I rubbed my mouth. "But not too well."

"Some of the county technicians do tend to rush. We'll ask them to take a second look at the Skulls."

"Why don't you do that?"

He paced in front of the desk, glancing at me, then at the dark enforcers.

"Mind telling me why I'm here?"

"It's been a dull week, and I've missed listening to your wit and repartee."

"I am in great demand, but my wit doesn't kick in until noon, and I don't do repartee until after five."

He stopped pacing and merely smiled. Ben is such a straight arrow that he makes monks look rowdy. He is also a master of the silence. In this age people are used to chatter, talk, music, and noise. People walk with headphones, drive with radios on, shop while music is blaring. Only a few, brave individuals want to be alone with their thoughts. So to sit in a barren room, devoid of sound, with an assistant state attorney staring at you with his perfect, gleaming White Shark smile can be unnerving.

Finally, I gave in. "Is there any particular subject you wanted me to be witty about?"

"The murder of Wes Meeks."

"I'm hearing that name a lot lately. That's no murder. He was in the killzone."

Ben's glimmer flickered hot and became his Old Testament righteous stare. Combined with his White Shark frown, it can prompt you to confess a multitude of crimes and sins. And that's when you're innocent. I imagine it's worse when you're guilty.

"The premeditated killing of a man, even a man like Meeks, is murder. The terms of killzone and liquidation have no basis in Florida law."

"A few juries have thought differently."

Ben didn't like that fact. Many cops and much of the public are ambivalent about Liquidators. Not straight-arrow Ben.

"Meeks raped and killed a young woman named Carla Martinez. He walked due to a technicality," I said.

"Murder is murder," Adonal said.

"I'm not mourning for Meeks. I doubt anyone is."

"Perhaps his father. It's said they were close."

"The fact that Merrill Meeks will get one less Father's Day card is no concern of mine."

"It isn't? Have an alibi?"

"Ben." I made the name sound like an accusation.

"You knew Meeks' victim, and you're a friend of her family."

I ignored the first part of his statement. "I am acquainted with her uncle, Art Sanchez. Acquainted with, not friends, although he's a nice guy. I see him about five times a year. Besides, even if I were a Liquidator, I wouldn't take this case because of that connection. I'd be the first person you'd suspect."

"So you don't have an alibi?"

I groaned. Still, I like Ben and cut him a lot of slack. Two years younger than me, he's the youngest ASA in the office, yet he takes the toughest cases. An idealist in a cynical age. A Christian in a secular age. A deacon at the Seven Oaks Presbyterian Church. He's also better looking than I am, but I try not to let envy curdle my opinion of him.

"As a matter of fact, I do. Newspapers said Meeks was killed early Thursday morning. Thursday around noon I walked into the Blue Ridge Genetic Clinic in Charlotte, North Carolina."

"Why were you there?"

"Thought they might need some help. They've been under fire from the anti-genetic Luddites. You know the slogans. 'Nobody should be genrich until everybody can be genrich,' 'Stop the genetic master race.' Death threats. Security problems. Things like that."

Adonal still smiled like a Great White. I wondered if there was blood in the water.

"You have to go to North Carolina to find work?"

"I'm working on a case and happened to be in the area. I stopped to see a friend of mine named Sierra. She wasn't there."

"Could you provide proof of this?"

I gave him my version of a White Shark smile. "Because of all the threats, the Blue Ridge Clinic is very security conscious. When I walked in, it took fingerprints and a retina scan. I went in a bit before noon. The night before a local motel has my credit card payment."

His smile shortened by a millimeter.

"Ben, if you don't believe it, hook me up to a TC computer and ask your questions. Truth or consequences. It won't beep."

"Great machines, but we can't use them in court yet. They're too new."

"Defense attorneys are fighting them. But everybody knows the TCs are 98 percent accurate. So strap me in and ask if I killed Meeks. The answer is still no. Am I sorry someone did? No. Do I know anything about the case? No."

Adonal took a deep breath. "I didn't think it was you, but I had to ask. We heard a rumor."

"A rumor I was involved?"

"Yes."

Mullet was right. Someone was trying to frame me. Mullet's credibility is not high, but the one time I hoped he was wrong....

"So that's why you used the Skullcrushers instead of calling my office."

"If someone thinks we've accepted that rumor, let them. It might give the investigators an edge. Word should get around rather quickly that the Skulls hauled you in here."

"The only person who could have started that rumor would be the killer, but Liquidators don't kill the innocent and they don't shift the blame to others."

Adonal still had his Old Testament glare. He added an accusatory snort to it. "You have a higher opinion of Liquidators than I do."

"I know you don't like them, Ben, but they have a code. I've never known one to violate it."

He walked around the desk and sat down. "A private firm provides the water system in this county. Garbage collection is run by a private firm too. Did you realize that?"

I didn't know if it was a question or a statement, and it came out of left field.

"Oh...ah...yes, I knew that."

"But society doesn't privatize justice," he said.

I spat a dollop of blood onto the handkerchief. "Private justice is better than no justice at all. Ask the Martinez family."

He didn't answer, but the laser stare didn't flicker or diminish. "Carter Dunlop. Could he be involved with the killing of Meeks?"

I shrugged. Dunlop is a much tougher, more lethal version of Mullet. He didn't run any scams, but he was for hire.

"He has a reputation, but he's not a Liquidator. You know something?"

"Dunlop is under pressure due to gambling debts—casinos and horse racing. For enough money he might do anything."

"He might, but so would a dozen other thugs in the area."

"Sorry about the Skulls, Jerico. We didn't intend to rough you up."

I shook my head. "Forget it. It goes with the territory."

The laser glare faded to low wattage—a sign the interview was over. Ben doesn't waste words.

When I walked outside, I hailed a taxi to drive me back to my car. I looked around before I climbed in, wondering if a strange pair of eyes was looking at me. Or a strange pair of sensors. I decided not to buy a lottery ticket. I figured this wasn't my lucky day.

Two

When I walked into my office I told my secretary, Helen, to hold all calls and told Francine, my computer, to distill all public information about the Meeks family. Helen nodded and pointed to my office. "You have a visitor. If you've had a bad day so far, she might perk you up."

There had been two surprises today, both bad. I was hoping for a good one when I opened the door.

Sierra Cassi, all five-feet ten of her, had her black boots on my desk. Her chair balanced precariously on two legs as she eased back and forth. Her orange skirt slid up and down on the light brown thighs. When she saw me, the chair slammed to the carpeted floor.

"Hello, Jerico," she said, flashing a big smile.

"Sierra," I said, emphasizing each syllable in her name. I moved warily around the desk. Usually, I'd be delighted to see a red-haired acquaintance, but this was not a usual day. I'd travel across several states to say hello to Sierra. She wouldn't walk across the street to greet me….. Well, maybe across the street and down a few blocks but certainly not over the county line.

"What are you doing here?"

"Sorry I missed you up in North Carolina. I'm visiting Daytona and remembered you have the best bourbon in the state. Have a glass?"

I walked over to the cabinet, took out two glasses, dropped some ice in them, grabbed the bourbon, and poured. As I handed the glass to her, she smiled. "Shouldn't I get a greeting?" she said. "Something like ' Sy, it's really good to look upon your sparkling, green-eyed frame. I adore you. You dominate my dreams.'"

"Ditto. Except I never liked the nickname Sy."

I sipped the bourbon. So did Sierra. Or rather Dr. Sierra Cassi, her medical certificate still being valid. However, she finds research boring so she moonlights in my profession, working for medical, genetic, or robotic facilities. Her reddish-brown hair flows below her shoulders. Her green eyes flicker with her 170-plus IQ. She looks frighteningly young. Thanks to genetics, she will look young for an amazing number of years. She has also used those young looks to great advantage.

"I'm sorry I missed you up in North Carolina too," I said. "But I assumed you were doing fine since you didn't call and ask for a song."

"You have a nice, soothing voice. Genetic or fluke of nature?"

I smiled. "Best I can tell, genetic fluke, although I do have one brother who's a good singer."

Occasionally, a dark, raging depression afflicts Sierra. She doesn't like taking the powerful drugs that will alleviate but not vanquish what Churchill called his "black dog." So she phones and asks for a song that will lift her spirits. The one wonderful thing about not hearing from her is that I know she's doing well.

"And what," I repeated, the taste of bourbon on my tongue, "are you doing here?"

"Vacationing. I'm going to the beach. This part of Florida is famous for its beaches. I'm also going to try to improve my golf."

"The last time you golfed you almost killed your playing partners."

"I did not!"

"You hit one with the ball and almost brained me with a golf club."

She raised her hand. "I was a little wild, but I want to improve."

She got up, held the glass, and walked around the desk until she stood by my chair. She wore a fragrance and a look that would make any robot wish he were human.

Sierra hopped on the desk, took another sip of her drink, then crossed her legs. The movement hiked up the already short orange skirt. The brown of her thigh was matched by the fraction of the darker brown holster not covered by the orange skirt. I figured she was about to tell me the real reason for the trip.

"Jerico, honey, stop looking at my legs. This could be important."

"I bet you tell that to all the guys."

"Do you know Alon Cheruba?"

I shrugged. "I know his name, but I couldn't pick him out of a crowd. He's a Liquidator."

She swirled the liquid around in the glass. Usually, tinkling ice doesn't sound ominous. This time, it did. "He's in the area."

This wasn't as bad as learning an alleged robotic assassin was after me, but I didn't think it was good news either. "Forgive me while I voice an old Southern expression."

Sierra snickered after the quick rant. "That's rather colorful, Jerico. I must remember it." She took a sip of her drink. "I gather Cheruba did not inform you."

"No, but I'm not a Liquidator. Even if he knew I lived here he was under no professional obligation to give me notice."

"Still, it would have been good-mannered."

"Right. Liquidators are known for that. And for always using the right salad fork."

Liquidators are a bit territorial. If they have a job near another colleague's residence, they let him know. Mafia hit men often do the same. It's a professional courtesy observed by men who don't usually follow other ethical niceties.

"By the way, is Cheruba genrich?" I asked.

"No, but don't let that throw you. He's amazing for being genpoor." She shook her head. "Genpoor folks are just a baby step beyond prehistoric men and women."

"Actually, some of my best friends are Neanderthals."

She flashed a patronizing smile at me. "I don't doubt that for a moment. Don't get huffy, honey. I wasn't speaking morally, I was speaking scientifically. Genetics is no longer a crapshoot. If you start life without being genrich, you're already behind the eight-ball. Other humans are vastly superior to you. Besides we need all those good genes. We have to deal with robots, synthetics, and all the new pathogens and mutated viruses."

And Jackals, I thought. "Sierra, I appreciate the information and it's nice to see you, but what's the real reason you're in Daytona Beach?"

She feigned shock and splayed her fingers over her heart. "Jerico, why would you say that? After all, you know my feelings for you."

"Er, annoyance mixed with a twinge of aggravation?"

She swallowed the rest of the drink. "Yeah, pretty much. But I wouldn't want anything to happen to you. I'd miss you, in a masochistic type of way."

"I'm touched."

She patted my chin. "You shouldn't be so suspicious. It's not becoming."

She hopped off the desk, walked back to her chair, and sat down. If she did have an ulterior motive for being in sunny Florida, she wasn't about to say what it was.

"Since you want to be of help, I can use your advice. Let me ask you something."

She nodded. I explained my problem and my morning conversation with Mullet. "So I can use your medical expertise.

If I took a bio-genetic Synthetic and crossed it with an advanced robot with Jackal mentalities, what would I get?"

"A very confused creation."

"Seriously."

"I am serious. Listen, the main advantage of Synthetics is they look and feel human...*are* human to an extent. But a medical Synthetic taking care of an elderly patient can't do much else. The sick and infirmed have someone to take care of them, touch them, give them human, or almost-human, contact at a low cost. But medical Synthetics are lost outside the house or the medical facility. I mean that literally. They might be wandering the streets in a daze. Of course, other types of Synthetics are used for, shall we say, recreational reasons by some rich old men. They're built for one function, just what men want."

"I've always enjoyed conversation too."

"Whereas the mechanics of robotics..." She began a detailed, scientific spiel until I held up my hand. She stared at me. "You were gen-rigged for intelligence, weren't you?"

"It's not my field."

"Ha! Your field is baseball and golf."

"Yes, and I'm proud of it."

"OK, we skip the robotics lecture, except to say they can't think and never will be able too."

"You realize some scientists disagree with you."

"Screw 'em. They're wrong."

"But—"

She cut me off with a flick of her hand. "Don't anthromophize robots, Jerico. A robot might beat you at chess but would never feel a sense of accomplishment. He could listen to a Mozart symphony and it's only a series of musical notes to him. Robotic software programming is rigidly logical. It has to be. But that means if a robot read the line, "I have heard the mermaids singing. I do not think they will sing for me," it means nothing to him because there are no such things as mermaids and, even if they were, they don't sing. You can't program in imagination."

I sipped the bourbon. "No souls?"

She shrugged. "No souls and no spirits. You can't get that in a lab."

"I see you're still a Catholic."

"Go to mass twice a week. Mass and your singing has helped me though many tough spots."

I thought for a moment. "According to Genesis, the duo God created in the Garden were perfect, right? No flaws, no sin."

"Yes."

"Speculate for me. You say it's impossible, but what if man could create something akin to life. After six thousand years in his fallen condition, what would man create?"

Instead of answering, she walked toward the portable bar. She set the glass down, then turned and stared at me. For a moment I thought there was affection in her eyes, but the stare became hard, and so was her voice.

"Something evil," she said.

Three

I switched to coffee while reading the documents Francine printed out. The Meeks family had established a reputation for both good and ill in this section of Florida. I had read occasionally of Merrill Meeks in the local newspapers and on the Internet. He attended some social functions and contributed to most of the local charities. The family went back about 150 years, which in Florida is akin to having roots in the Reformation. The original Austin Meeks popped up about the turn of the twentieth century and made a fortune in real estate, citrus, and insurance before marrying when he was close to fifty. His son Roland added a few shopping centers and condos to the family fortune. Roland's son Terrill basically kept the fortune together. Great-grandson Merrill reorganized the family business and created the St. John's Foundation, a medical nonprofit that did genetic and robotic research. Reports said it was a top-of-the-line facility that could even do cloning, if the law had allowed it. Which meant it could also produce Skullcrushers and Guardians...or Jackals.

In past years, I had played poker with Merrill. I never liked him, but he was a bad poker player, and those are the type of people you want at the table. Merrill reminded me of the old-time, rough-edged, good ol' boys who helped build Florida during the early decades of the 1900s while also enriching themselves. Cunning, with a certain business savvy and a greedy vision of the future, they helped claim the state from mosquitoes, swamps, and alligators. A few were honest. A few were visionaries. More than a few had one or more skeletons in their closets and committed a few felonies on their way to becoming respectable.

Wes Meeks was the black sheep of a family already tending toward dark gray. Two assault charges—one dropped, probation for the other --- over the protests of Ben Adonal. At least one rape charge was also dropped, no doubt because the family paid the victim an incredible large sum of money. Then came the attack on Carla Martinez.

Wes was pictured with his father in a few stories. Average height, chubby, with full cheeks, but an amiable smile, and short hair. Nothing in his looks suggested a predator. He was genrich, but somebody omitted the conscience gene when they fiddled with his DNA.

I wanted more information. As it happens, I am a paid-up member of the Daytona Beach-Volusia County Chamber of Commerce. A few years ago I did a little unofficial work for the chamber. Several prominent members were almost burned in a shady land scheme backed by one of the directors. The director was quietly sacked and the chamber breathed a sigh of relief. The members showed their appreciation with generous donations to the charity of Jerico Drake, Inc. During that time I met the organization's vice president, Arturo Donovan. While a nice guy, Arturo has the traits you'd expect in a chamber vice-president—friendly, personable, charming, and he will talk your ear off. He can spread twenty seconds worth of information into twenty minutes. I wondered if listening to Arturo was worth any life-saving information he might reveal.

I decided yes, but it was a close call.

I timed Donovan. It took him thirty-seven minutes and thirty-five seconds to impart all his information. Summing up, most of the unsavory rumors about Meeks were true. He never let ethics get in way of profit or of his ambition, but he was also careful. Nothing too far outside the lines. Meeks took pride in his heritage, regaling friends with tales of his father, grandfather, and great-grandfather in the early days of Florida. But, reproductively, he may have been flawed. He had wanted sons from an early age, but there were two marriages without issue. Then in his early fifties, his third wife produced a son, and a year later, a daughter. Meeks cared little for the daughter, but doted on his son, the inheritor of the Meeks line. Although genrich, Wes was not a brilliant example of the new genetic technology. His intelligence wasn't impressive, he had little charisma, and he tended toward flabbiness. But Merrill didn't care. As long as he had a son to continue the Meeks line, he was happy.

About a decade ago, Meeks announced plans for the St. John's Foundation. There were other partners, but he was the major investor. It was surprising to friends because Meeks was tight with a buck and had never before expressed an interest in science.

"But he could always spot trends," Donovan told me. "He can be crude, even vulgar in his conversation. If you focus on that, you don't realize what a clever mind Merrill has. He went in on deals no one else would and made them work. He backed out of deals that others were eager to invest in, and he was usually right. Whatever else you can say about Merrill, he can think ahead."

Since the murder of his son, Meeks was depressed and in isolation. There was now no heir to the Meeks legacy. Wes was twenty-four when he died, which would make his father seventy-six or seventy-seven.

"An old seventy-six or seventy-seven," Donovan said. "Merrill drove his life on full octane, and now there's nothing left but the fumes."

And, perhaps, a desire for revenge before he trudged into the great beyond.

Four

I flipped a page as Helen rung me and told me my appointment had arrived. I had almost forgotten her. I asked Helen to bring her in.

Lori Hollendorf walked in smiling, although she didn't have a great deal to smile about. Just nineteen, her violet eyes flashed with the vitality of youth. She was slender and small-boned, with a petite nose and mouth. Excellent figure. Not stunning, but definitely cute. She was dressed in smug brown slacks, a yellow blouse, and a tan vest that matched her perfect, tanned complexion. I didn't know if I felt joy or discomfort because she bore an ever-so-slight resemblance to a young girl who made my heart skip a beat when I was a high school junior.

Ms. Hollendorf is among the genrich generation. My genes were sculptured, but the techniques were fine-tuned by the time she was born. The slang term for my genbatch is "genplus." Not as pathetic as the common folk, but not as superb as the genrich generation who came a few years after us.

They are a new breed of young people: incredible IQs., anti-aging genes, athletic skills, superb immune systems. I assumed my client made straight A's in biology, chemistry, genetics, advanced calculus, history, English and, for all I knew, mechanical engineering. She probably also played the "Moonlight Sonata" skillfully and composed violin concertos. It's all in a day's work of being genetically enhanced. Many humans look at the genrich with apprehension. Since this is the first generation, society still doesn't know how they will respond and react as adults. They hold popular culture in disdain. Of course, any intelligent man or woman would. It's rumored they look askance at the human race. But if so, who could blame them?

There's only one drawback. Their immune systems are so powerful, our lethal, virulent STDs take much longer to kill the genrich. Average men and women, when infected, last four months. I've heard a few genrich individuals have taken two years to die, although they spent the final six months wishing they were in the grave.

Being genrich has solved one of the age-old problems of teenagers. No skin problems. Science is still defeated by the mouth ulcer, but it has conquered acne. For the 15 percent of teenagers who are genrich, liberation day had arrived.

"Miss Hollendorf, please sit down."

"Did you find anything, Mr. Drake? Please call me Lori."

"Yes and no. Yes, there was something unusual about your brother's death, but, no, there is no concrete evidence of foul play. The North Carolina investigator handling the case was away when I was up there, but I talked to some of her colleagues. Your brother was a healthy, somewhat athletic thirty-one-year-old who apparently slipped off a ledge and fell 150 feet into the gorge below. There were no drugs or alcohol in his system when he died."

"Cary drank moderately but didn't take drugs."

"I went out to where he fell, looked at the house, checked out the spot where he went over. There are no antigrav devices there, not even any guard rails, so a fall is possible."

"But not likely." The 180-plus IQ gaze darted up and down. I had the feeling she was a female Ben Adonal in waiting.

"No, but if such events were likely, they wouldn't call them accidents. However, there was something else. Black Mountain is not a big town, but they do have a excellent forensic scientist in Asheville, which is about ten miles from it. There were some contusions and abrasions on your brother. He hit on slanted ground and rolled, but there was one mark or bruise that the pathologist didn't think came from the fall." I pointed toward the back of my neck. "It was here, along the neck and upper back. It...."

"As if someone hit him to send him over, Mr. Drake?"

I nodded. "Yes, and please call me Jerico. The pathologist believes this abrasion came before the fall. It's not enough to base a murder case on, but it's enough to keep the investigation open."

She thought for a moment. "There were a number of people saying nasty things about my brother."

"Yes, but English teachers or writers don't generally kill over literary quarrels, and none of them happened to be near Black Mountain, North Carolina, when your brother died."

Cary Hallendorf was a brilliant historian/biographer who had won critical applause and bitter condemnation in his brief thirty-one year life. Although only genplus, he had the wide-ranging intellect of the genrich. At twenty-two, he published a biography of Edgar Allan Poe that critics praised lavishly. Intermixed in the biography was a literary critique of Poe's stories and poems, along with the author's learned opinions on how the specific incidents in Poe's life influenced his writing.

His next book, published when he was twenty-six, was *Wesley and Whitefield and the Seeds of Change.* Some historians believe without the Great Awakening in the 1730s, there would have been no American Revolution, and there would have been no Great Awakening without John Wesley and George Whitefield. Lori's brother had chronicled the lives of the two preachers and established—beyond the doubt of most critics—that there was a direct connection between their preaching and July 4, 1776.

Due to his success, there was already some resentment in academia of him, but it was his next book—a collection of a dozen critical essays—that unleashed the literary knives. He took six best-selling books, eviscerated five of them, explaining precisely why they were useless as literature. One, though, had literary merit and he effectively praised the book. Of the other six essays, five did the same critical surgery on books that had been widely applauded by reviewers and academics. They were as bad, if not worse, than the best-selling pulp, Cary Hallendorf concluded, writing that the authors added pretentiousness to their execrable prose. Surprisingly, *At the Garbage Heap: A Look at Modern Fiction* was moderately successful, making the best-seller list for ten weeks. While his literary opponents might overlook Hallendorf's criticism, they could never forgive his success. He received angry e-mails and a few death threats.

For his next project, he turned back to biography and started research on author and essayist Munson Cain. Cain had published three noteworthy books early in his career, wrote several flops, then turned to political writing. He won new fans and became a darling of much of the cultural elite by advocating his particular brand of political and sexual nihilism, with dark undertones of violence. He was famous for a fictional passage that described—then lauded—an assailant who knifes and murders an elderly store clerk. The attacker was authentically human, Cain gushed, in a society that had become too roboticized. Striking out against the robotic culture meant you had to strike out against humans as well. Such violence helped make us authentic because it brought an element of danger into life, and only humans, not robots, can ever feel danger. I thought this infantile but many social and cultural critics lapped it up. Elderly now, Cain had been in the shadows for a few years, occasionally popping on a talk show to spout his views. Cain had houses on both the east and west coast, but also a cabin near Black Mountain, where he kept many of his papers and correspondence. Hallendorf had been doing research at Cain's house when he fell into the gorge and died.

"I still want you to stay on the case," Lori said.

She reached in her handbag and pulled out a packet of medical cigarettes. She took one out and tapped it on the chair's armrest. I stood up, walked over and flicked a lighter. She held the cigarette to the flame.

"Isn't science wonderful? We've got good genes and those are beneficial," I said.

"Yes. After Cary's death I went into an emotional tailspin. My doctor recommended them. I have one last pack left. I have a hard time believing they were ever bad for you. Still, it's rare to have a man light a woman's cigarette nowadays. Chivalry seems to have died out."

"Yes, about five hundred years ago, but I'm leading a Renaissance."

She laughed, then leaned back in the chair.

"Lori, I don't want to leave any false hope with you. If this was foul play, it will be difficult to prove."

Her sparkling eyes dimmed briefly, the golden vibrancy of youth changing to the grim gray of human experience.

"I understand, Jerico. There are no false assumptions here. I want you to continue the investigation. Cary was a great brother to me. When I was nine, Cary was twenty-one and working on his first biography. He was up in Vermont. It so happens I love skiing, snow skiing. He called our parents and said, 'Send Lori for a month. She'll love it here." He lived close to a ski lodge. They did, and I enjoyed the best January of my life. I was on the slopes every spare moment. That was the type of brother he was. He could have spent his time on his book or with girlfriends or just on his own life. He thought of me. How many brothers would have bothered with a younger sibling?"

"Certainly not mine," I said.

"Oh. Brother or brothers?"

"Two older brothers. One sister a year older. But I was genrich—we were still called genrich back then. They demoted us when I was about sixteen to genplus. But being genrich basically isolated me in my family."

"I'm sorry to hear that, but I've known other genrich students who've had that experience. The interplay of genrich people with their environment and their family is one area that interests me, and one reason I'm pursuing psychology. Another few weeks and I'll have my degree. I'm in my fourth year at Florida." She raised her arm. "Go Gators!"

"You'll have your degree that soon?"

She shrugged. "Some genrich kids already have their college degrees at my age. I took it more slowly. It's not that impressive."

"It is to me. But I'll take the case pro bono. I hate to take money from a struggling college student."

She tapped her cigarette ash into a black ashtray on my desk. "I'm not that struggling. Cary made money from his books and I'm his heir. Our parents died tragically three years ago. A boating accident. They married late. I came--unexpectedly but they told me happily— when mother was forty-seven. No childhood trauma here. I had a very happy childhood."

"Wish I could say that about mine."

"So there's no need to cut your rates."

She stuck out her hand. I shook it.

"I want a resolution to this. For some tough years when I was adjusting to my genrich status, Cary was my lifeline. I don't want a question mark hanging over his death. I miss him. As I said, I had a tough time when he died. I haven't completely bounced back, emotionally." She stubbed out her cigarette, then leaned back in her chair. "There's no one to talk to now. Genrich individuals have trouble relating sometimes. I... this is going to sound snooty. Got acquainted with a guy recently. He seemed interested in me, but he didn't know who Beethovan was. Never heard a symphony. I like Eliot too. His poetry is incredibly rich, and the guy said, 'Who'? Plus, he had no interest in learning who Eliot was. So I said, "This isn't going anywhere." Her fingers were on the tobacco tip of a second cigarette. As she brought the filter up to her mouth, the eyes widened with alarm. She blushed. "Oh, I'm sorry...that does sound awful. I just.... I'm not saying if anybody doesn't know who..."

"I have heard the mermaids singing, each to each. I do not think that they will sing to me."

Her smile nudged the room temperature up a degree or two. I lit her second cigarette.

"Thanks. Another Eliot lover?"

"I'm not as enthusiastic about him as you are. That particular line is familiar because it was recently misquoted by a friend."

She gave me the Ben Adonal stare, with feminine intensity. Her laser glare wasn't as white-hot, but it was more focused. For an edgy moment, I felt she could peer into my past and see the weaknesses, the flaws, the failures. A personality was being peeled away as she dug into the emotional core. No pretensions, no rationalizations. Just a bare human soul. My spinal fluid became an ice stream, with brooks flowing around the chest and shoulders. I shuddered with the cold. Then she smiled and the ice melted.

"I was told you believe in good and evil, that wrong should be righted, that the guilty should pay, and that justice should be done."

"That pretty well sums it up."

She stood up. "It was not mentioned that you are rather handsome."

"Due to excessive modesty, I ask people to leave that out. Were you told anything else about me?"

She nodded and gently pressed two fingers to my chest. "That you have a good heart."

"Were there any dissenting votes?"

She chuckled but the laughter turned into a deep sigh. “I’m a Christian, Jerico. I don’t want revenge, but I do want the truth. I want to know what happened on that ledge.”

Her genes were not the only thing that made her different. Most people would want revenge if their brother was murdered. I would want revenge. Well, not for my brothers, but the general idea is sound.

She directed one last stare at me. I wondered if, somehow, my character was being weighed. I must admit I was curious how I’d stack up. Which way would the scales tilt?

“You have interesting eyes, Jerico,” she finally said.

“Are they sparkling and mischievous?”

“No, they’re deep and, I think, wise, but somewhat sad. I’m guessing they’ve seen a great deal, not all of it good. Your soul has experienced much. How old are you, if I may ask? About Cary’s age?”

“A couple of years older. We were in the same genplus batch.”

She blushed again. “Forgive me. Since Cary’s death I tend to go off on tangents. I’m better than I was but sometimes...”

I smiled. “This wise, experienced soul understands.”

And it also thinks you have talent as a psychologist, I thought.

I watched her leave. She was among the best and brightest the human race would ever produce, yet that was no guarantee of happiness or a life without tragedy.

A Christian. She shared more with Ben than just a stare. Two of the Lord’s righteous.

There are some who think the Old Testament God was harsh. He smote too many people, according to modern critics. I always thought that was a point in God’s favor. My problem with the Almighty is not that he smites people from time to time. I only regret He doesn’t do it more often.

Five

There was a midnight flight out of Jacksonville to Charlotte, North Carolina. It didn't take long for Francine to drive me to the airport. Some individuals, men mostly, prefer to grab the wheel themselves. Other individuals have almost forgotten how to drive. I drive manually occasionally, but usually let Francine do it. She follows maps a whole lot better than I do.

I eased behind a round dark table in the airport lounge after purchasing a ticket. I smiled when the flesh-and-blood waitress approached. Airports do not like robot waitresses. Robots are good for all manual labor jobs such as citrus worker, fast-food staffer, gardening, or garbage collection. But waitressing is one of those jobs needing a human touch. This waitress was tall and dressed in red. Sparkling gold strips lined her burgundy pants and red sleeves. She showed why the human touch is needed by flashing a dazzling smile. Her voice gushed with excitement. She scribbled down my order on her green, rectangular pad. I watched her walk away, the rump firm in the red pants.

The noise of passengers and friends floated through the lounge: random talking, a shout of recognition, a groan of a missed connection. Two men browsed through the paperback stand, figuring which book to take along on the flight. The square black robotic cleaner rolled noiselessly through the terminal, snatching every bit of litter and waste. Occasionally, it would hum and stick out a hose to vacuum a chair or an airline counter rug, then snap it back. A mother with a baby sat almost alone in the long line of blue chairs in the terminal. The child was asleep, but the mother looked a bit despondent, glancing from one end of the building to the other. Her legs rested next to a plaid overnight bag. I had taken one sip of my drink when she jumped up and embraced a man. He mumbled apologies for being late, kissed her, and then gazed lovingly at the child. He grabbed the overnight bag and they walked out, arm in arm, the baby still sleeping soundly. He would wake up in a crib.

The waitress returned and asked if there was anything I needed. I said no.

My next visitor did not have a smile on his artificial visage, nor did blood run through his robotic circuits. Waitressing and greetings are handed by humans. Not security. Or not by humans alone. When I had bought my ticket, my name flared orange on the computer list, meaning I carried a gun and should be questioned. If my name had flashed red, a Custodian would have zapped me, taken my guns, and carried me to a small interrogation room to wait for his human boss.

Instead, the Custodian gently grasped my forearm and escorted me to the interrogation room. I smiled and walked with him. It's not advisable to give Custodians any trouble. In a half second a robotic grasp can become paralyzing. No one wins lawsuits nowadays because they were inconvenienced or even treated roughly at airport terminals. Not anymore. It's a different world now. But we don't lose any airplanes.

Custodians are almost as big as Guardians and almost as mean as Skullcrushers. Their color is not the hard black of the Guardians, but a less intimidating gray. Their flaming crimson eyes have intimidated more than one man. Even humans with nerves of steel have been known to visibly shake when a piercing robotic gaze is directed at them. Custodians are polite, but they don't take any guff. I showed the gray shadow my identification and my concealed weapon permit.

The Southeast Security chief was a barrel-chested, large-nosed man with squinty eyes, a black crew cut, and a expression that read ex-cop. He looked as comfortable in his job as Einstein must have looked at a blackboard. Although made of flesh and bone himself, I gathered he surveyed all humans with suspicion. Can't say I blame him.

He flipped my I.D. open, stared at it, then at me. A Custodian was beside him. I sat in a chair in his office.

"You carry two guns, Mr. Drake?"

"I always like a backup plan."

He grunted.

"One time a man holding a gun on me patted me down. He missed the beretta in the ankle holster. Always figured it might come in handy again."

"What happened to him?"

"Doing twenty to life in Raiford."

I saw a hint of a smile. He looked at his robotic colleague. "His prints and scans check out?"

"Yes, sir. He is Jerico Drake. His guns are registered."

He nodded and tossed the I.D. back to me. "OK, then he's fine. Let him board. The company has sky marshals. If one is on the flight, I will inform him about you, Mr. Drake. Wouldn't want him to get nervous."

Two days later, I sat at a motel poolside table drinking coffee with Detective Jacylyn Henderson. She had the professionalism of her airline security colleague but a charming smile. The sun bounced yellow lasers off the flowing blue pool waters The wind blew fiercely, splashing water over the walls. A huge, green umbrella shaded us.

"I'm sorry I missed you, Mr. Drake. When you were up here before, I was over in Charlotte, testifying. A murder trial was moved due to excessive publicity."

"Get a conviction?"

"Yes, we did."

"I appreciate you talking to me. Many police officers don't like private detectives."

"I make my judgment depending on the detective. You're looking into the Cary Hallendorf case?"

"Yes. And please call me Jerico."

"I'm Jeri. Similar names, almost. Why are you interested in Hallendorf's death?"

"His sister hired me. She's curious."

"So am I. But I can't prove anything."

"Any suspects?"

She sipped the coffee and gave me the cop look of inspection. I must have passed. She set the coffee cup down and smiled. "The subject of his biography."

"Munson Cain?"

She nodded. "Cain was the last person to see Hallendorf alive. It's estimated that Hallendorf fell or was pushed off that ledge around nine. Cain claimed he left the house around seven, drove to the airport—or had the autocomputer drive for him—and took a ten-thirty flight to New York. It would take about seventy-five minutes to drive from the house to the airport. Nobody remembers seeing Mr. Cain until shortly before he boarded. He said he was in the airport bar drinking. Of course, there are two major problems with Cain as the suspect."

"I can think of one," I said. "Isn't Cain almost eighty now? So how did an eighty-year-old man toss a thirty-one-year old genplus biographer over a cliff?"

"Exactly, although Cain is only seventy-seven. However, he had two hip transplants recently. When I saw him, he was using a walker. That makes it even more unlikely that he's the murderer if, in fact, Hallendorf was murdered."

"What's the second problem?"

"Motive. I can't for the life of me think of why Cain would kill his biographer. The guy loves publicity. He'd open his own cable network if anyone would watch."

"As a biographer, could Hallendorf have uncovered something that Cain wanted kept secret?"

She gave a harsh, bitter laugh. "I can't imagine what that would be. Cain has been married five times and strangled his third wife, or at least tried to. Fortunately, other people were in the room and pulled him off. She didn't press any charges. After the assault, his status in the literary set went up. Cain later remarked that if he had killed her, book sales would have skyrocketed. The thing is, they probably would have. What could he possibly have in his background that he hasn't already revealed and written about? After he wrote his three major novels and a couple of flops, he began penning semi-fictional autobiographies until people got sick of reading them. He would have turned any scandal into another best seller."

"So there's no motive?"

"Besides pure meaness, no."

"Mean? I've read where he's a charming fellow, one-on-one."

"If you don't happen to be an ex-wife, maybe so."

"Any other suspects."

She shook her head. "No. No suspects, no motives."

"But the case is still open?"

"Yes. Until I'm satisfied, it will be."

I nodded. I needed another plane ride.

Munson Cain had a house on the Massachusetts coast. The waves moved lethargically, but rhythmically to the shore, but Cain was in no condition to enjoy the scenery. We were on his open-air porch, with brown, wooden beach chairs beneath us. Wind-blown sand scattered across the burnt-wood furnishing of the floor. Cain sat beside a Servitor, who helped him when he walked. He held a drink in a tall, yellow glass. I had remembered a picture of Cain on the back of one of his books. But it must have been one of his earlier novels. He was leaner back then, and the hair was darker.

At seventy-seven, he still possessed a magnetism, and dark flashing eyes, but the flat stomach had rounded into a beer belly. About five-eight, the pronounced belly gave him a short, squat look. The once dark hair was streaked through with gray.

Salesmen and exceptional con men often have charisma but they focus on you. You believe they care about you, want to hear your problems. They say soothing things when you tell them the minor irritations of your life. They outshine you, but the listener is convinced he is the center of their attention. Not so with Cain. I sensed he wanted to be the center of every conversation, if he wasn't talking, that is. He cared nothing of the concerns of his audience; they were merely ears to hear him. His personality was akin to a wave washing over you. You no longer cared about your vague irritations. You only wanted to flow along with Cain. His voice was the only tone that mattered. Other people were secondary and unimportant. His words flowed smoothly. The twin currents of arrogance and egotism converged to form a rushing stream. Many had been swept along in Cain's verbal tide.

"Tragic, tragic," he said, swirling the liquid around in his glass. "You hate to hear of any person's dying but especially a young, creative man. Cary was brilliant. I read his first biography and thought it magnificent. Didn't read the second—I'm not a religious man and have no interest in those who are—but I did read his third. The literary crowd attacked him for it but, most of the time, he was right on the mark."

Cain took a swig of his drink.

"You were apparently the last person to see him alive."

"Yes, we talked and spent some time out on the ledge. I had to go back on the house and sit down, due to my legs." He tapped his thigh. "Can't stand up anymore. I overdid after the operation and wound up back in bed. The doctors put me on a strict regimen and—" he jerked his head toward the robot—"I have Hiram here to assist me. He helps me walk when I need it, but he also puts me through my exercises. You can't argue with a robot. Actually, you *can* argue with them. You just can't win the argument."

I nodded. "I was injured about three years ago and was in rehab for a couple of weeks. If the doctor orders twelve specific exercises a day, the medic robot has you do twelve—not eleven, not thirteen, but twelve. But there's no choice about those twelve."

"Yes. Fortunately, I did all of mine before you got here. If not, Hiram would have interrupted our conversation and hauled me away to the exercise room."

A breeze rustled his curly hair. He smiled at me, but there was a suspicious glare in his eyes.

"I checked out the ledge on your Black Mountain house and noticed there were no antigrav devices or even guard rails."

He gave a derisive snort. "Munson Cain with guard rails? Never! My critics would never let me hear the end of it. I've lived dangerously all my life and now I'm expected to put up guard rails? I'd rather go over the side of a cliff."

I wondered if I should point out that strangling a woman who weighs seventy pounds less than you do is not all that dangerous, nor is it courageous. But I was here as a detective, not as a cultural critic.

"You kept papers at the Black Mountain home?"

He nodded. "Until recently, I had an apartment in New York, this house, and the one in Black Mountain. But the New York apartment was too busy. I could never get anything done.

When I wanted to do some serious writing, I went to Black Mountain. It was my Cuba. Hemingway loved Havana, but the Black Mountain home was always a good place for me. A lot of my papers, e-mails, and correspondence was there, some initial drafts, a computer I used, things like that. Cary was going through stuff I had long forgotten. I was glad he was doing the biography. Nowadays, I'm pretty much ignored. A biography would get me back in the limelight."

"He was a literary critic too. He might have been tough on you."

He drained his glass and shook his head. "I've got three books that will stand the test of time and the toughest critic. A lot of people say my political essays are crap—"

"I think 'rantings of an infantile ego' is the more accurate quote."

His river flow of words halted. His lips curved downward, revealing a jagged tooth. He didn't like criticism that scratched his ego. His voice dropped. "You've read some of my detractors. There's a lot of envy and fear mixed in those reactions. We live in a sterile culture, Mr. Drake. Sterility and conformity destroy the imagination and the creative impulse."

"You advocate violence to overthrow this alleged sterile culture, but violence is never creative nor imaginative."

"If that violence leads to a society where we can become fully human, it would be worth it."

"Your critics call you selfish and narcissistic."

The laugh had a bitter edge to it. "They've said worse things than that. But I have three books that put me with Hemingway, Faulkner, Joyce, Bellow, Algernon. There's not many in that circle, but I'm there." He tapped himself on the chest. "Munson Cain is among the greats. *Green Dust at Evening, A Sad, Eloquent Morning* and *Grave Near a Second-rate Road* have been praised by the best of critics. I had no worries about what Cary would say about them. In fact, talking with Cary has stirred up my creative juices again. I plan to head back to Black Mountain soon. I think I have another book in me, and I want to get back to writing."

The literary world would be thrilled.

"You left Cary about seven the night he died?"

He swirled his head around, as if he had a crick in his neck. "Yep. I was coming back up here. Thank God for autocomputers. With my legs I couldn't have driven, but the computer got me to the airport. The service robots helped me the rest of the way."

"You told the police you went into the bar?"

"Yes. I told them I sat in the lounge drinking until the flight took off. But I think I had one drink, then walked to a small store, bought a paperback and read it. Wasn't very good, though."

"Remember what it was?"

He shrugged. "Some mystery novel, but as I said, it wasn't very good. Some mystery writers are worthwhile. A few get down to the grit and brutality of a culture. I wasn't impressed with this one, though. Can't even remember the name of the novel or the writer. I think I threw it away before I got on the plane."

Convenient, I thought.

"So have you turned up anything in your investigation?" he asked.

I did not like the quick flash of darkness in his eyes. Deeper than his normal color. A spurt of black. Of guilt? Or of wariness? Could Cain feel guilt?

"Not yet, although there are a few odd things I'm looking into. It's difficult to believe Hallendorf simply tripped off that cliff."

"Sad. Very sad."

I couldn't tell if he meant the death of Hallendorf or the loss of his biography.

"The '60s. I would have been at home in the '60s," Cain said.

"We're not there yet," I said, puzzled by his statement.

"No, I meant the 1960s. There was a revolution and rebellions against the prior sterile decade of conformity. I would have been part of the vanguard. I've read a lot about that period and I feel a kinship with it. Perhaps with a few more like me, that revolution would have succeeded."

"We've done all right."

He shook his head violently. "In our little enclaves we are the '50s again, the 1950s. Sterile, conforming, routine..."

He stopped talking when he noticed my frown. "You disagree, Mr. Drake?"

"Yes. Many of the people in the 1950s had lived through the Depression and fought in World War II. If you have to scramble for food, then fight in Europe or on a Pacific island to save civilization, you're entitled to a peaceful decade. You're entitled to a peaceful life, for that matter. Plus, in that decade, they laid the groundwork for the Cold War, which defeated another evil in the twentieth century. That's an impressive achievement. How many people critical of the '50s ever had to work ten hours a day just to get grocery money? How many critics risked their life on the beaches of France or on some godforsaken island in the Pacific?"

I gave him an I-think-you're-an-idiot smile.

"Our balkanized culture is an affront to morality. We have re-segregated into white sections, black sections, Hispanic areas, elderly enclaves. The genrich are moving to isolate themselves from the rest of the society."

"You have a nice little enclave here. I don't see you giving it up, or moving to a minority area."

"This is a stale-white-bread society. It's not conducive to creativity—or to mental health, for that manner."

"In the 1950 the crime rate was much less than a decade later. People fulfilled their dreams, accomplished their goals, and were able to walk down the street at night in peace. I don't see that as a bad decade."

He stiffened and gave me a wary glance. "We have different views, Mr. Drake."

"We're different people, Mr. Cain."

I let the autocomputer drive me to yet another airport while I smoked a cigar. Cuban variety. The best in the world. I like the long, thin ones. I had the same problem as Detective Henderson. I didn't see how an enfeebled, aging author could have pushed Hallendorf over that cliff. Or what his motive might have been.

But I didn't believe him.

Munson Cain was lying.

I was sure of that.

Six

As the jet circled Daytona Beach I watched the azure waves crash onto the beach sands. I caught a glimpse of the ten-story Bahama Hotel where Sierra was staying. The day was incredibly sunny, but the plane's atmosphere was a comfortable 72 degrees. The hum of the air vents acted as a tranquilizer.

Glenda, the blond flight attendant gave me a merry smile. "Good to see you again, Mr. Drake. Did your business go well?"

"About as well as I expected."

No robot flight attendants. A robot can't comfort edgy passengers or smell of purple lilac. Couriers look human and can pass for flesh-and-blood if no one has an extended conversation with them. In talking, Couriers don't convey real emotion. Any laughter is hollow. Since they have no emotions, their speech is stale and flat. The robotic mind can't grasp the concept of humor or sarcasm. Neither can robots pat you on the shoulder as you walk down the connecting corridor and wish you a good day. Well, I suppose they can, but Glenda does it with utmost sincerity.

At my house, I didn't have to check the security systems. Francine does that. It's not as easy to kill someone today as it was fifty years ago. Back then, if someone was determined to murder you, the odds were on the criminal's side. After you were dead, the killer might get caught and convicted, but that was of cold comfort to the victim. If the would-be victim lived in an area with strict gun-control laws, the odds shifted even more dramatically for the killer who would not, obviously, be worrying about possible handgun violations. Now with Guardians, the odds have shifted to the law-abiding citizen. It's difficult to bring a Guardian down. A single bullet won't do it. A full clip from a small hand gun might, if the shooter gets lucky. A couple of rounds from a .357 magnum will do damage. If Carla Martinez had had a Guardian around, she'd be alive today. But she didn't know she was in danger.

The house was secure. Francine controls several lasers set on stun. Perhaps she can't think, but if someone tried to break in, he'd be stunned instantly. The office is similarly equipped. So if someone, or something, tried to kill me, he or it would have to carefully pick the time and place.

The phone buzzed and the smiling, larcenous face of Mullet popped up on the screen.

"Jerico, buddy, I have some information for you."

"Someone else wants me dead?"

He shook his head. "Nope, but I found out something about Meeks' murder."

I was waiting for Mullet to name a price, but he didn't pause for a commercial message.

"Meeks wasn't killed instantly. He was hooked up to a TC computer before he was murdered."

"What?"

"No question about it. When you're on a TC, it leaves residual traces. Around here..." He traced two small circles on his temples. "Microscopic but measurable. Someone grabbed him, hooked him up, and started popping him with questions. The machine beeped at least once before Meeks was killed."

"Why would anyone ask questions of Meeks?"

"That I don't know, buddy."

"A Liquidator wouldn't do that. He's beyond asking questions."

"Maybe it wasn't a Liquidator. Or maybe this one wanted to know something."

I thought for a moment but came to no conclusions. "Thank you, Mullet."

"I didn't ask for any cash upfront. I trust you. Pay me what you think it's worth. I have one thing more for you."

"Please continue."

"You may have a couple of days. There's been some problems with the Jackal."

Maybe Sierra was right after all.

"It may not be ready yet," Mullet said.

"You know when it's set for a trial run?"

He shook his head. "Not for sure. The info is tough to get, Jerico. I'm not swearing 100 percent that it's accurate. There's an outside chance the Jackal is prowling, but there's a better chance it's still parked in the garage."

The screen dimmed and went blank.

"Francine."

"Yes, Jerico."

"Transfer a thousand dollars into the account of Melvin Arthur Dubose. You have his account information. We've done business before."

What type of information would a killer want from Wes Meeks? I didn't have a clue. But I did have an idea of how to find out.

Art Sanchez was in the restaurant business. He owned three and they all did good business. He was usually at his downtown establishment. El Charro was two blocks south of city hall, and many city employees walked down for lunch. Mexican-American cuisine. A waiter directed me to a small table in the back. He brought a glass of water and set it down on the silver tablecloth. I sipped it. A few minutes later Sanchez came and sat down across from me. He's a middle-aged man, genpoor, going a bit stout in the waist. Sun-tanned brown but with white, jagged teeth and a crooked smile.

He wasn't smiling today but he did managed a half-grin.]

"Jerico, how've you been?"

"I've had better days."

The half-grin disappeared. "So have we all."

I sipped from the glass again. "You have good water, Art."

He shrugged. "Everything here is good. We're famous for our clam chowder, best in the South. Our key lime pie has a well-deserved reputation. Much better than those people down in Key West make. The finest sirloin on the coast too. Artificial now, of course, but you can't tell the difference." He gave me his half-grin again. "What can I do for you? You didn't come to discuss the menu. I appreciated your sentiments after Carla's death. So did the family."

"That's what I need to talk about. Art, a Liquidator killed Wes Meeks."

"He got what he deserved."

"So he did. I won't argue that. But the rumor is his father believes I killed Meeks and has hired a hit man."

Sanchez shook as if a gust of wind hit him.

"Art. I know you and your family. They would not want to cause trouble for an innocent man."

Sanchez was silent for a moment. His eyes narrowed. He scratched the corner of his lip. He shifted in his seat, then edged forward. "I regret to hear that. Our family holds you in high regard, Jerico. Obviously something like this was not expected...but what can we do?"

I smiled. "I think you can help me out. Before Wes Meeks was killed, the Liquidator plugged him into a TC computer and asked questions. I want to know what Meeks answered." I raised my hand to cut off Sanchez's remarks. "Don't say anything. Just listen. If anyone in your family has knowledge of who killed Meeks, they can contact him and open a channel for that information. A Courier would be perfect,"

Sanchez sat back. He gave a slight nod. "But even if the Liquidator could be contacted —in theory of course—he would not have to go along with any suggestion, even of his former employer."

"No, he wouldn't. But Liquidators don't make trouble for other professionals. It's part of their code. He might well agree to share the information."

Sanchez thought for a long time. He sat so immobile I wondered if I should call the EMTs to check his heart. Then the corner of his lip flickered slightly. He gave an almost imperceptible nod.

Seven

I was planning to call Sierra but she called me first and requested a song. She didn't smile. Depression dimmed the flashing eyes.

"You're not supposed to be depressed while in Florida. It's against state policy, and the chambers of commerce get all upset. They sell the state as a panacea for all mental ills."

She forced a wan smile. "Sing to me, Jerico."

I have to be careful. No love songs—none of a man singing to a woman. It makes her uncomfortable. Civil war tunes are theraputic, as are Irish ballads. Gospel songs are also powerful antidotes.

I cleared my throat and hit the right key.

"Hold back the river,
Push back the tide.
Climb every mountain.
Push every fear aside.
Jesus is the answer..."

I gave a ten-minute rendition before I saw her smile. The strains and stresses on her face slackened. She sighed and shook her red hair. The strands that shrouded her face were whisked away and the lively Sierra returned.

"Want to have dinner? I need a bodyguard."

She smiled. "Not tonight, Jerico. That was a bad one. I'm going to stay in. Maybe listen to some music. Thanks, though. I love your singing."

Honey, if you'd let me, I'd serenade you every night.

Lori was pleased with the invitation for dinner at the Orion Restaurant. I promised I would brief her on my trip to North Carolina. The Orion has a five-star ranking in all the tourist manuals. I think the rating has more to do with architecture and aerodynamics than food, although the latter is excellent. I explained there could be a slight element of hazard but that, too, seem to intrigue Lori. Genrich individuals grow up quickly. There was no reason to be diplomatic with her.

"So do you expect people to open fire on you at the restaurant?"

"No, or I wouldn't invite you. If Jackals are like human killers, they will watch their victim before deciding on the perfect time and place. It would have to be someplace away from security cameras and lasers, although possibly a Jackal wouldn't mind the cameras. A laser could stop him, though."

"Let me guess." She hummed slightly when she was thinking. She brought a finger up and slowly tapped her lips. "You are being stalked by an unknown robot assassin, but you don't mind going to dinner. The Orion is a first-class restaurant, and no doubt has first class-security, with possibly a few Guardians on staff."

"Not possibly. That's a certainty."

"So if someone—or something—looked suspicious and tried to enter the restaurant, they'd stop him or it or a combination of both. The Orion would also have security lasers strategically placed."

I nodded.

"But the...shall we call him Jack? Jack the Jackal?"

"As good a name as any."

"Jack would need to know about you, your movements, your habits, your hobbies. Not everything is on file or on the Internet, not even in this day or age, so he might want to watch you to seek out a vulnerable area."

"Yep."

"But you don't know who Jack is. He could look human, like a Courier. So you want to draw him out. If someone is stalking you and follows you to the Orion, you want to have people watching him and trailing him."

"Lori, I hope whoever is after me is not nearly as insightful as you."

She smiled. "Doubtful, and that's not a boast. Even our advanced robotic software is quite limited in its own way. If you tell robots the alphabet, they can go from A to B to C, but any type of creative thinking is impossible. Jack would have to follow up, watch you, to build up his alphabet data base. If he leaves out a letter, he's lost."

"Are you sure you're nineteen, or just a young-looking fifty-nine?"

She laughed. "It's the former, although at my age you want to be older. Young people want to be older, older people want to be younger. Nowadays, you can be much older and look young. I may study that too. What's the psychological effect of being thirty-five and looking only twenty-one. Of being forty-five and looking twenty years younger."

"Kinda creepy," I said. "But since I'm talking to a genius, perhaps I should put that in more scientific jargon."

"Yes, the correct scientific phrase is skin-crawling creepiness. We must be accurate."

A coastal establishment with tables not just on the oceanfront, but also above the waves, the Orion has received the highest ratings from all the best restaurant critics. Long, plastic pilings curved to form elegant stems, whose flowers became round tables bedecked with deep blue tablecloths. In white letters, Orion was spelled out in old English letters on menus. Aircarts equipped with antigrav devices brought waiters and trays. About two dozen tables were outside, with others inside for those diners who found eating directly above the ocean unsettling. Dancing was conducted on rounded orbs, some large enough to accomodate several couples, others with room only for a duo. At night, soft blue and green lights lit up the watery arena. For those who were careless, had too much to drink, or were simply lousy dancers, there was a thin, soft filter net two feet above the ocean. It was flexible enough so that dancers who tripped would spring back up, unharmed. A few were so spritely that they bounced back to their dancing platform, a feat always applauded by other dancers.

Two dark Guardians stood on each side of the silver door as we drove up, but the parking attendant was human. He smiled graciously as I dropped the keys in his hand. A rather antiquated gesture since cars can pull themselves into the parking slots, but such pedestrian antics are frowned upon in establishments such as the Orion. The human touch is preferred.

The red eyes of the tall Guardians flared as we approached. They emitted an angry hum. I slid my hand into my pocket and brought out the identification. One Guardian curled black fingers around it. I explained I was licensed to carry guns and slipped my hand onto the identiplate. It flashed green. The Guardian moved aside.

"By the way, any robots allowed in?" I asked.

"Only if they are used as bodyguards, sir."

I looked at Lori. "Just checking."

We rode an aircart to our table. The sea rolled gently below us. The waves sloshed against the pilings.

"Would you like a drink?"

"I think I would like to try something. Can you suggest one?"

"A sloe gin fizz for the lady," I told the waiter. "I'll have a whisky sour."

I saw a flash of alarm in Lori's eyes, so I quickly said, "They're non-alcoholic these days. You can swallow a dozen and not get drunk, or even tipsy. They taste like the original drink but have the kick of Ginger Ale."

"Actually, once Gingle Ale put me under the table. Aren't there some clubs—"

I nodded and smiled. "There are places that serve the original hard stuff. Many men, and some women, like to go to them. The Orion is more high class than that. Only the best for you."

She laughed, but still changed the order to pink lemonade. The evening sky darkened. The blue and green lights flowed over the table like a gentle wave. A caressing flash of green embraced the contours of Lori's face. She wore a bright orange evening dress and dazzled me with her smile. A blue necklace graced her throat. The dark eyes held a quizzical look. I couldn't quite read the expression. Some men would have assumed it was sexual longing. An uncontrolled ego will make those mistakes. The ego is the same, whether the human is genrich or genpoor. It can trip you up and make you act like a fool. Lori placed her elbows on the table, folded her hands and placed them under her chin.

"May I ask you something?"

"Sure."

"When I went looking for a detective, I asked around."

"My pic on the Web site didn't pull you in?"

"It had a magnetic effect, but I still wanted background."

"A wise decision."

"I didn't ask just people who liked you, I made sure I talked to at least one person who didn't like you. It's always good to get both sides. So I found one person who was not a friend of yours and he said you had any number of flaws."

"How long a list did he give you?"

She laughed. "Long enough, but he said something that puzzled me. He said it was dangerous to get you angry."

A low growl rose in my throat. I drowned it in water. I usually ignore what people think about me. For some reason, I cared this time. I didn't want Lori to think the description was accurate.

"Only to criminals," I said. "The person you spoke to was probably referring to two incidents in school, one in junior high."

"Please tell me about them."

"Before dinner?"

The waiter brought our drinks and set them before us. Lori drained some of the pink liquid from her glass.

"Yes. Please."

The tone was between a request and command. Even though I, surprisingly, wanted to explain, the latter caused small ripples of resentment. The human ego is odd indeed. I took a sip of my drink before answering. "When I was in fifth grade, a bully named Jason made life miserable for me. He was a year older, thirty pounds bigger, and stronger. He terrorized a lot of kids, but picked on me because my father was rich. I came home with a lot of abrasions. Couldn't sleep, couldn't eat, because I worried about Jason. Grades went down that year. Next year he went off to junior high and I breathed a sigh of relief. However, our elementary was next to the junior high. A couple of walkways connected the two schools and we shared grounds. I saw him occasionally when I was in sixth grade, and he promised to make life miserable for me the next year when I moved to the junior high. That thought sent chills down my spine.

"So I went to my father and asked if I could take martial arts classes. I expected he would ignore me or tell me he was busy but, for once, he listened, then asked why I wanted to enroll. With Dad time was precious—he always had business deals rolling—so I spoke quickly, rattling off the fifth-grade problems and saying I'd be seeing Jason again in seventh grade and I wanted to be prepared. He said, 'Yes, you have to take care of yourself.' Then he enrolled me in a gym that had Tae Kwon Do classes. That was in May. For the next four months I was at the gym at least four times a week. I also, and I don't think this was entirely the result of the training, had a growth spurt that summer. In sixth grade I was smaller than the average student, but that summer I put on about forty pounds, and none of it was fat. I also grew three inches. When school opened in September, I was ready. I wanted to meet Jason again.

"I didn't have to wait long. On the first day of school he was picking on some other student. I told him to stop. When he saw who it was, he smiled. I still remember that smile. Gleeful, and a bit sadistic. I had grown, but I'm sure he remembered that small kid back in fifth grade, and that's who he saw. He said, 'Or what?' and shoved me hard. I let myself fall. He gave a harsh, guttural laugh. I turned over, and used my hand to push off from the ground, On the way up I clenched my fist, turned and swung from the heels. Caught him square in the jaw."

Even today I smile when I recall the incident, although I hoped the grin didn't look malicious.

"Knock him out?" Lori asked.

"Almost. His heels met air. He fell hard. When he got back up, he wasn't sure where he was. His fists were up, but he wobbled on rubber legs. Kept planting his feet as if the ground wasn't solid. I feigned a punch to his head, then hammered his belly button. Drove it back into his spine. Before he went down, a tooth flew out when I pounded his jaw. I knew he was down for the count so I headed for his companions. Bullies usually have scum around them. One was a fat kid. I knocked the air out of him. The other guy took off running. Jason was still on the ground, and not going to get up any time soon. Grabbed him by his shirt, pulled him up, and *wham!* Picked him up and punched him again. The last time I grabbed him by his hair, pulled him up, and told him if I ever again saw him bullying a boy, girl, animal, or insect, even the best medical attention in the state of Florida wouldn't fit bones back into joints. Dropped him and he hit the ground with a thud."

"You get suspended?"

"Surprisingly, no. I listened to the principal ramble on, then held up my hand. Gave him a cold look and said, "Mr. Nettle, that—and I won't use the word I used in the principal's office—used to beat me up regularly in fifth grade. I imagine he did the same to others here. I'm guessing this is not the first time he's either been in this office or a subject of conversation here.' Nettle blinked and twitched his lips. I knew I had hit home. Then I told him, 'With all due respect, sir, I've just solved your problem. He's not going to cause you any more trouble." One reason, of course, is he'll be a while getting out of the hospital.' " Lori snickered, turning her head to hide her laugh.

"That was his response," I said. "Although he tried to stifle his laughter. I told Nettle, 'Even when he gets out of the hospital, he's not going to bother anybody anymore.' Troublemakers know the system because they have so much experience with it, and Jason knew the system couldn't do too much to him. Now he knows there's a penalty for misbehavior. Education will improve this year.' "

"What did the principal say?"

"Not much. He thought about it for a while. Then said, 'You can go back to class now.' When I got home I went to my father, told him what happened and said I appreciated the gym membership. He said, 'I'm proud of you, son,' and went back to work."

It was the only time he said he was proud of me, and the only time he ever called me son.

"Thankfully, there are robot monitors now in the few public schools we have. Public education is on the wane. My parents wanted a public education for me, and I stayed until the third grade." She shook her head. "It was just too slow."

"It wasn't designed for genrich students. Better to study at home."

"You mentioned a second incident in your junior year."

I sipped my whisky sour. "You don't want to know about that."

She removed her straw and placed it on the table, then brought the glass to her lips. When she lowered it, a thin pink line ran above her upper lip, a shade lighter than her lipstick. She wiped the line away with a napkin.

"Yes, I do," she said.

I paused. I was not particularly ashamed of the incident, but not proud of it either. I let Lori take another sip from her drink before talking.

"At our school, one boy had been in a fire. He had had several operations, but his face was still scarred, He had several more operations scheduled. He also had a understandable phobia about fires. One day, a random bully was chasing him down the halls. The bully had a lit cigarette. He threatened to squash it in Billy's scarred, pink face. When I caught him, we were near a staircase. I tossed the smoker down the landing. He smacked against a cement wall and fell back across the stairs. I ran down, grabbed him again, and bounced him down the second flight. To make a long story short, two of our school's linebackers had to pull me off him."

I waited for a reaction but got none. She took another sip of her drink while her gaze remained steadfast on me. For some reason I felt uneasy. I never thought a teenager could make me edgy.

"I'm not like that anymore," I said quickly. "The army trains you to keep your emotions under control. Never get angry. You'll make a mistake and get killed, or you'll make a mistake and kill someone unintentionally."

"How long did you serve?"

"Three years."

"Forgive me if I ask one question. It will sound insensitive."

"That's okay. My profession isn't known for its sensitivity."

"The training? They taught you how to kill?"

I grinned. That was a common mistake of civilians. "No, they taught me to stay alive. You don't have to be trained to kill. People do that all the time, every day, with no training at all. Back at the turn of the century, twelve-year-olds shot their teachers and six-year-olds shot other students. Selfishness and murder are innate in the human race. Original sin, maybe. Cain was the first murderer and he never received any training. It just came natural to him."

"Did you see combat?"

I nodded. "When the Muslim nations in Africa declared jihad on their southern neighbors, we went to their aid. Then went up to protect what's left of Europe from the jihadists, but that was settled without military action." I knew what her next question would be and thought I would answer it. "Yes, I killed a number of men."

She signaled to the waiter for a second lemonade. We were silent as he brought her another tall glass. She sipped it while the violet eyes studied me. The glare continued for about a minute, then her lips parted in a smile.

"I liked and admired my brother. We disagreed on some things but there was a wonderful bond between us. He was a truly extraordinary man. Although I think you're the right man for this case, I don't think Cary would have liked you, Jerico."

"Well, ma'am, some people don't."

"But I like you."

I smiled.

The waiter brought the main course.

While she munched on the prime rib, she talked about her brother and his gentleness and kindness. Unlike many brothers who might be consumed with sibling rivalry, the twelve-year-old Cary was delighted at the arrival of a younger sister. Her first memory was awakening from a bad dream, perhaps when she was three or four, with her brother lifting her into his arms. She must have cried out in the night and he hastened to her bed. It was a vague memory involving some black monster chasing her, then safety as her brother held her and made her laugh. She fell asleep in his arms with the monster put to flight.

It was Cary, a senior in high school, who accompanied her on her first day of school. And it was Cary who helped her grapple with her high intelligence, a trait that separated her from most of the other children. Because of her brother and her parents, she never felt alone in the world and always felt confident she would not only cope but triumph. She appreciated the affection and returned it. She encouraged Cary's literary pursuits and was thrilled when his books won critical acclaim.

Ironically, her parents had reservations about genetic therapy. They were concerned the procedure would produce another fission line between humans. Scientists were, in effect, creating not a different but certainly a better strain of humans. This was in a time when balkanization had already split society, creating white, black and Hispanic zones. The elderly lived behind high walls. Her parents wondered if society needed another artificial barrier but, finally, did not refuse the technology. Cary was genplus and Lori, when she was born, was fully genrich.

As we drank the restaurant's rich, aromatic coffee Lori asked if I knew who my shadowers were. I gave my best guess and pointed to a middle-aged couple a few tables down. With the dim light, the man looked stout and balding and the woman appeared not to have benefited from altered genes. Cosmetics, I told Lori. I'm guessing they are both very young, quick, and good with guns. With the pilings in darkness, their table seemed to float in the air, a single light in the middle. Several couples were on the oval dance floor, or dance floors. One lady in a green evening gown slipped and fell into the blackness. Her yell was more of laughter than shock as the net caught her. She bounced once and plopped on the strands. Her legs went through the loose net, two feet above the flowing waves. Shark fins had been seen in the waves at one time, and became a big attraction. Customers loved brushing the firm fin as it passed beneath them. Then the owner admitted the shark was artificial, but that revelation didn't cause any loss of interest in the aquatic attraction.

Lori said her brother talked about his work but didn't mention anything specific about the Cain biography.

"He was a tireless researcher. He ran down friends, relatives, lovers, the waiter who served Cain one day in a California restaurant." She sipped her coffee. "He was hunting for anyone who knew anything about a Smokey Lansdale, who is dead now but apparently had a dramatic influence on Cain."

I shook my head. "Haven't heard of him."

"I think Cary mentioned Lansdale died about forty years ago, but he did think Lansdale was pivotal in any story of Cain. Cary seemed very excited about his discovery."

"Did he say who Lansdale was?"

She shrugged. "Early literary influence. Strangely enough

Lansdale was from the South. Cain was born in New York. I don't know how they connected."

I took her hand and led her to a dance cube. For some reason, I didn't expect her to be a good dancer, but the genrich are often athletic and graceful. When I twirled her, she delighted in skirting the edge of the orb, swaying and swinging hips and legs, challenging the darkness. I gripped her hand while she whirled around the circumference, punctuating the dance with an occasional kick. The soft blue and green light accentuated her dress. Her necklace flashed blue lasers at me.

Later, my hands around her slim waist, her hands around my neck, intertwined with the thick hair, we scooted around the circle.

"Like to be serenaded?" I asked.

"You sing, too?"

"In my high school, I was part of the Four Tenors."

"Jerico, you're a baritone."

"Yes, but there was some flexibility with the membership."

She gave a hearty, joyous laugh. "I haven't had this much fun in months. It's been a sad time since Cary's death. By all means, sing a serenade."

"In my travels, I have roamed,
"Near planets a thousand
light years from home."

"A beautiful song," she said.

The song lists the splendor of the universe but ends with the claim that "nothing matches the beauty of your eyes." I think I missed a note toward the end.

"That's all right. I loved it," Lori said.

I got the call when I was driving her home.

"Yeah."

"Mr. Drake. I'm with the Conklin Detective Agency."

"I was expecting your call."

"No one is tailing you, sir. No one followed you to the restaurant or is trailing you now. You're clear."

"Thank you. I appreciate it."

"Just in case, we will follow until you reach your house. We give full service, sir."

"You do good work. Thanks, again."

I smiled at Lori. "It was just us tonight."

Eight

She lived about five miles west of Ormund Beach. A split-level, older house with a driftwood fence in front and a wire one in back. Lots of yard.

"Why don't you come in a minute? I make a great cafe Caribbean."

She unlocked the door, then told me to stand still. I heard rustlings and movement inside. Then she beckoned to me.

"Walk slowly," she said.

I stepped gingerly onto a thick blue carpet. As I walked into the room I saw two huge German Shepherds sitting like two bookends, eyes wide, noses pointed at me. Both gave a throaty growl, not menacing but noticeable.

"Hi guys," I said.

"This is Duke and Dixie," Lori said, scratching both behind their ears. "They are my animal companions. I love dogs."

"So do I."

I offered both hands, palms down, and smiled. They trotted over, sniffed fingers, then legs. Both were black with silver streaks. I had no doubt their genes had been altered to heighten their intelligence. They were at least as smart as dolphins. Duke sniffed around my right knee. Dixie lifted her head and looked at me. Lori disappeared into another room.

"Have a seat, Jerico," she said.

The dogs escorted me toward a green, cushioned chair. Dixie gave a joyous yelp, jumped, and placed her front paws on my chest, then licked my chin. Over Dixie's elongated ears, I saw Lori come back in with a silver coffee tray.

"Dixie, get down! Sorry, Jerico. I forgot to tell you when Dixie likes you, she makes her affection known."

Does her human companion do the same? I almost asked.

I petted Dixie as she eased down by my chair. Duke sauntered over and sat next to Lori.

"They are beautiful animals."

A gold frame encased a poem on the wall. I walked over and saw "The Hound of Heaven" in ornate, old English type. Lori smiled when she saw me reading it.

"That is a sentimental favorite. It's not in the Eliot class, but I still love it."

"No, it's not in the Eliot class."

"Still, the analogy is wonderful. God is like a hound. He eternally pursues the sinner, never giving up, always ready to snatch him from the jaws of hell." She smiled. "We had golden retrievers when I was young. We'd toss a ball or rubber plate and they'd go after it. When I was seven or eight, I'd thought it would be fun to retrieve things too. So for a while I ran with the dogs. Whoever got to the ball first would run it back to Mom or Dad."

"So you became one of heaven's hounds."

"Since I believe in heaven and like dogs, I consider that a compliment."

She handed me an orange cup of aromatic Caribbean cafe. She returned to her chair and crossed her legs. I noticed the tiny security laser at the corner of the room. Probably another was behind me. Nowadays, even without huge German Shepherds, a modern home is a very secure place. The tiny green spot on top of the laser blinked. Green designated stun. Some homeowners have their defenses on kill. It's legal and has reduced home invasions.

"Jerico, may I ask you one more question?"

I smiled and nodded. Her question was a sword and it scratched the corner of my smile, drawing blood.

"Do you have any idea why the real killer singled you out as the possible Liquidator, and why people would easily believe that?"

"Those are two questions," I pointed out.

The violet Lori-stare sent blue flares my way. She sipped the coffee and grinned. A dark drop smudged the top of her pink mouth.

"You don't waste your genrich status, do you?" I said.

"That would be a shame."

"I am not a Liquidator, Lori."

"A certain assistant state attorney I questioned was adamant about that, but that doesn't answer my question."

"He is another hound of heaven, saving sinners if he can. Convicting them if he can't. Of course, I deal with sinners too."

"Yes. I prefer Christians myself."

"I hope I'm the exception to that."

She sipped from her cup. "Well, you're not a Christian, but I don't think of you as a sinner. Not totally. But you haven't answered my question."

"It is well known that I am sympathetic to Liquidators."

The statement hung for a moment like the cream in the coffee. I felt obligated to explain. I wanted the weight of her disapproval off my shoulders.

"Wes Meeks raped and killed a woman named Carla Martinez. Meeks was not a person who would ever feel shame or guilt. His actions did not bother him. Since he can't feel remorse, he should feel fear. If Meeks was still walking around, I don't think he should strut with the knowledge of his crime, but step anxiously because he doesn't know what's around the corner. He should be afraid every day of his life. He should live with fear. If you tell a rapist or killer that a Liquidator is on his trail, they begin to sweat and shake. It's a rough type of justice, but justice nonetheless,"

She swirled the coffee in her cup. "Is that all?"

"Well, there might be one other, small item."

She nodded for me to proceed.

"Some years ago I knew Carla Martinez."

"Knew?"

"In the biblical sense."

"Oh." She packed a lot into that one-syllable word.

"We found out very quickly that we did not click. The chemistry was okay, but other aspects of the relationship were not. But we stayed friends. She was a wonderful lady. So I was angry when Meeks got off. A day or so after he walked, I was in a bar, and had at least one drink too many. I made some statements that Meeks and his father could have interpreted as threats on his life."

Lori set the cup down. She placed her elbows on her knees and leaned forward. The purple gaze flared and became a darker violet. Her dagger-sharp voice impaled the words in my mind. "Were you planning to kill him?"

I took a deep breath and eased back into the chair. "You don't even have your degree yet."

"A mere formality."

"It's a moot point. Wes Meeks is dead, and I did not liquidate him. But I'm not sorry he's in the cemetery."

She leaned back in her chair and recrossed her legs.

"I'll go now." I put the coffee cup down and stood up.

Lori walked toward me. There was an ottoman next to a large chair. She leaped on it. With the ottoman's inches beneath her feet, she was close to my height. She grabbed my chin and kissed me affectionately.

Then she smiled. "No, Cary would not have liked you, but I'm glad you're around."

As I entered my house, Fred from the Conklin Detective Agency called again and assured me I was not being tracked. I petted my two Alaskan Huskies, then walked out on the beach. The waves lapped quietly on the shore. I looked around in the darkness, but everything was calm. Possibly, the Jackal wasn't ready yet. If I were planning to kill someone I would wait and watch first. Plan a time and a place. It was the intelligent play, for man or robot. Tonight I would take Fred's word. I didn't think he was a man who made mistakes.

But the Jackal was out there somewhere, waiting.

I shrugged. I supposed I could go to Ben with my information.

Say Ben, why don't you get a search warrant and turn the St. John's Medical Clinic upside down? I think they have an A.I. robot who is planning to kill me.

Sure, Jerico. Get a search warrant to inspect a respected scientific establishment built by a prominent citizen who gives to charities and has won the chamber of commerce's "Man of the Year" Award because of the word of a criminal lowlife and known liar.

Mullet has been right occasionally.

So he tells you a Jackal is after you, although there is no evidence that a Jackal has ever been built in any lab in the world.

Well, it was just a suggestion.

I would have to handle this on my own.

Nine

Some dreams leave you with the night jitters and a case of the yips. Sweat pours out and runs down your chest and there's the smell of fear when you wake. Other dreams leave you with a profound sadness, an aching loneliness as sharp as broken glass across skin.

The first type brings you awake with a start. A split second after waking you're sitting up in the bed, heart racing, prepared to fight the night demons. After the second type, you wake exhausted. Even if it's a sunny morning, there's a grayness around you. The first type are more dramatic, but the second has longer lasting effects.

The kitchen's bright lights didn't dissipate the dream gray. Coffee percolated as I poured orange juice into a small glass. I felt my way around the table, grabbing cabinets and chairs to make sure I didn't fall.

"Francine, anything on the perimeter?"

"Nothing, Jerico. It's a quiet day. My sensors tell me there is nothing unusual in the area and no strangers roaming."

So I didn't bother to pick up a gun before I strolled out onto the beach. The fresh air made things better. A jog might clear the mind. But not until I returned to pick up a weapon. A jog would take me beyond Francine's sensors. Run down the beach after a bad night might bring an even worse day. A sniper in a tree...

I shook my head. *You're getting paranoid.*

"No, I'm not," I said aloud. "There's a mindless, soulless

creature out there who wants me dead, plus a few flesh-and-blood humans who would enjoy reading my obit. Just because you're paranoid doesn't mean you don't have enemies."

I returned and picked up the beretta and shoved it into the jogging pants. Jocque and Jackie yelped with excitement, then joined me in my run down the beach.

When I got back, sweating with the effort, I told myself I might ask Lori about the dream. She was majoring into psychology. Perhaps she'd taken a few courses on dreams.

After I showered and ate breakfast, I begin tracking down English Lit experts, narrowing the list to three by mid-afternoon. The first one was on a sabbatical in Europe. The second, Dr. Lasley Barret, was a professor at Florida Atlantic University who specialized in twenty-first-century American literature. I phoned him and, fortunately, caught him in his university office.

He was a pear-shaped man, the abundant middle narrowing from small shoulders and a head that seemed like an ellipse on top of a circle. In a world where many men had broad shoulders and narrow waists, his physiology gave him a uniqueness he probably didn't enjoy. He looked uncomfortable in his body but warmed when he spoke of his specialty.

"Munson Cain. A fascinating writer and individual. Due to some of his outrageous behavior and comments, some critics downplay the brilliance of his early novels because they detest him personally. Others praise his later novels and political work because they like him. Both are wrong. The trio of Southern novels is brilliant. Most of his other work is trash. The political essays I can't comment on."

"I gather most of his life is known."

Barret sniffed as if a bad smell was in the room. "Almost all of his life is known, including his views of his fifth-grade class. Cain's favorite subject was always himself. Most of us know much more about his life than we care to. In my classes, we focus only on his three good novels."

I asked if he would be kind enough to summarize his lectures while adding any relevant biographical material. He startled me with his eagerness. Perhaps too many students fell asleep in his class. He knew I would be an rapt audience of one.

Some fifty-plus years ago, Cain had already published two novels and was getting a few good notices. The two early novels were flawed but showed much of his prodigious talent. The better critics said the young novelist needed to discipline his enormous abilities. At times his egotism ruined passages and plots. The narrators of both novels was a man similar to Cain with toned-down versions of his own egomania.

Then while touring the South, Cain met John "Smokey" Lansdale, a writer and poet who had grown up in south Georgia and had published a half dozen stories in regional magazines. One of Cain's good traits is he promoted other, less-well-connected writers. Although the two were very different, they became friends. Cain sent one of Lansdale stories up to the *Maine Literary Quarterly*. The magazine never passed 25,000 in circulation but had enormous influence in the literary circles of the northeast. Lansdale's story was well received, and soon other literary outlets began seeking stories from him. The fame was short-lived. Five months later, Lansdale was killed in a motorcycle accident. Cain was devastated.

"It's unfortunate that the funeral for Mr. Lansdale was not taped. It is said by many in the audience that Cain gave an eloquent, poignant eulogy to a friend. It was probably the finest speech he ever made, and free from the alcohol-induced stupors that would affect later public appearances. After the death, Cain surprised almost everyone by purchasing a home in North

Carolina close to where Lansdale lived, and cut most contacts with his literary circle. Eleven months later he produced his first good novel, *Green Dust at Evening.* The influence of his dead friend was undeniable, and he dedicated the book to Lansdale. In the novel, Cain had imposed tight discipline on his writing. The prose was strong, controlled, yet flowing. Cain dropped the first person narration and, surprisingly, made all his Southern men and women come alive. It was brilliant. It was also rumored that when he was writing the book was the only time when he did not drink, or inject illegal substances.

"Two years later he released, *A Sad, Eloquent Morning* to even more good reviews. There were occasional spots when the old Cain appeared—ranting, egotistic, sloppy—but for most of the book he again channeled his talent and produced an exceptional novel. His third novel of what came to be known as his Southern trio was two-thirds brilliant but also disappointing."

"Why disappointing?"

"A few of the more perceptive critics wondered how long it would be before the old Cain took over. His sloppiness took over the last hundred pages of *Grave Near a Second-rate Road.* A few of his solid, three-dimensional characters began to preach and rant. Another character, who looked suspiciously like a fictional Munson Cain, was dropped into the novel and began spouting nonsense, although all the other men liked and all the women admired the fictional Cain. The plot unraveled and became silly and irrational. Many college classes read two-thirds of the novel and stop.

"After those three novels, Cain degenerated. The rest of his works is awful narcissism. He still has talent, but he simply doesn't have anything worthwhile to say. His fiction after the Southern trilogy is embarrassingly awful. It takes a great talent to write that badly. After those three books, he focused most of his energies on his political essays. Perhaps he realized he could not improve on his Southern trilogy and didn't try. Besides they made him a wealthy man. All were best sellers and optioned to Hollywood."

"Weren't Hemingway's earlier books his best?"

"Yes. Another example of wasted talent. He, too, had control of his subject matter in his earlier works and he influenced literature for fifty years. But he lost his talent in his race for machismo. There are some similiarities with Cain. In their later works occasionally you see a flash of brilliance, but not often."

"How would you sum up his political philosophy?"

"Cain has no political philosophy. His personal philosophy is that of a spoiled six-year-old. Boiling it down, it's basically, 'if it feels good, do it,' no matter if such behavior is selfish, sadistic, and violent."

I thanked him.

I took a cigarette from a green pack with an oasis on its cover and stuck the filter in my mouth. My mind turned back to the dream. With the dream came the premonition again—the cold, dark spectre that first arrived on a warm, sunny day.

The sun had eased beneath the horizon, but the day was still golden. We had been dribbling and shooting. Now half the sun was blocked by the basketball backboard. The shadows darkened the ground. I was alone, staring at the hoop, with the graying sky in the distance. I had cast the thought down before, or ignored it. The spectre had no power until that day. It hovered around like an angry, hungry dog, nipping at my mind. When I slapped it away, it howled and fled. But the snarling canine was always on the periphery, waiting for an opening. Yet it wasn't snarling that day. The knowledge came as the sunlight diminished. It was absolute and unavoidable, stark but not horrific. I did not tremble or shutter. No goose bumps appeared. Just a sadness and a bleak recognition of what was to come.

The spectre whispered to me that I would die young.

And I knew it was so.

There could be no protest, no denial, and no hope.

When I was in an African forest, bleeding from a jihadist wound, one of the reasons I was so inwardly calm was I knew it wasn't the time. I could still die. Deaths and tragedies occur in life, but it wasn't the day of my destiny. The spectre, with icy breath and graveyard delight, had mentioned my appointment in Samarra. But it wasn't time, not yet.

I snubbed out the cigarette and lit another one. The robot servitor rushed over and emptied the ashtray, depositing another one on the table while he washed and scrubbed the first.

Over the years, the premonition just grew stronger and, with the dream, was stronger still.

I stood up and walked to the picture window. The sun was bright on the blue waves. A few stragglers strolled down the beach, smiling and laughing. I shook my head to get the premonition out of my mind.

The hologram appeared, as always, out of thin air. She was almost six feet, with red hair, sparking green eyes, and a beckoning smile. Long, brown legs. Clad in a silver teddy. She reached out for me, and her soft fingers touched my cheek.

"Jerico, you are troubled. May I help?"

I smiled. "Not today."

"I can change. I can look like..."

"No, thank you," I said sharply.

She smiled back at me and disappeared.

Yes, you could change. You could become Sierra for me. Or Lori. Or the friendly, smiling high school blond sophomore who moved away mid-year. At one time I thought your warmth could melt the icy spectre. But you, dear Holly, are artificial, and the spectre, though intangible, is all too real.

Of course, the house is almost totally self-contained. Set the security cameras and lasers and ask Holly back. Relive the glory days of the military. Kill only holographic enemies. Sing the glory songs and swap lies. Play Pebble Beach. Win the Masters, Just a command away. Then celebrate by making love to Helen of Troy. You're genplus, better than 99.99 percent of the human race. Rapidly become obsolete due to the new genrich batch of course but....

Yes, Holly. Just you and me. Rather you/Sierra/Lori/Helen and me.

Then I, my dear, would become as artificial as you.

Ten

I swung the six iron, then heard the perfect pitch of contact. *Smack!* The divot erupted into the air, then fell gently back onto the green fairway, The golf ball soared high and straight, then moved right as my hook took hold.

"Not too much," I said,

Sierra had her hand near her yellow cap, blocking the sun's glare. She whistled with admiration. The ball hit the green with a thump, bounced once, and rolled toward the cup.

"Slow down, slow down," I said.

The ball ignored me and kept rolling, ending up about twenty feet past the red and white flag. I looked at Sierra. "The greens are fast."

"Darn good shot though," she said.

I eased back into the golf cart as Sierra revved the engine and drove us down the asphalt cart path. She wore a white sleeveless blouse and a short orange golf skirt. Her left hand was stuck in a pale yellow golf glove. "So what am I doing wrong?"

"You have developed one of the traits of new golfers, and many old ones. You're not keeping your head down. Golfers who are anxious to look at their shot will glance up too quickly. It throws the motion of the swing off and the club doesn't hit the ball solid."

Her ball was about fifty yards off the green. She had hit the rough on her drive and pitched the ball back in the fairway. She stopped the cart and fished her pitching wedge from her bag. "I'll remember that."

Her gloved hand squeezed the club. She looked toward the green and made a practice swing, the club swishing through the grass. The ball would need to hit on the first cut of the green so the momentum would carry it to the cup. Any less and Sierra would be left with a long putt. Any more and her ball might end up behind mine.

She kept her head down this time. The wedge caressed the ball, picked it up gently, and bounced it on the target spot. The ball weaved right, then left, and rolled to within six inches of the cup.

"Yes!" Sierra yelled and gave a victory salute.

I missed my birdie putt when the ball rimmed the cup.

"So what's your handicap now?" Sierra asked while driving us to the next tee.

"Handicap? Bite your tongue."

"Whoa. You've gotten better. So when do you turn pro?"

"If I were good enough, I would. Could you imagine making a good living by knocking a little white ball around?"

"Probably be nice, but I like what I do."

I adjusted my cap, then looked at her. "That brings me to the next subject. What *are* you doing down here?"

She gave me a baffled look. "Playing golf?"

"Yes, but when I was walking to the clubhouse, there was a man walking out. I didn't think I could pick him out of a crowded room but perhaps I can. It was Alon Cheruba."

"Does he play too?"

She halted the cart at the next tee. I stepped out but rested by arm on the hood as I stared at her. "Not as well as we do. After all, he's genpoor. All the best golfers are genrich nowadays."

"Don't underestimate him."

"What other things besides golf are you playing? It's not just a friendly question. I'm in the middle of something, and I find it rather odd you're down here at the same time. We're friends, honey, so level with me."

She paused, then patiently marked her scorecard. She stuck her foot on the dashboard, took off her cap, and swung her hair. "I'm investigating the theft of items and information from the Blue Ridge Genetic Clinic."

"Someone down here took it?"

"Possibly. The Jacksonville-Daytona Beach-Orlando triangle is a base for a great deal of medical and genetic research. Some of it fits hand-in-glove with research down at the Cape."

"What type of information?"

"Information that could be used to assist in cloning. And, I suppose, information that could be used in building a Jackal."

I took a deep breath. I took out my driver and made a practice swing before answering. "I thought you said building a Jackal was impossible."

"I still think it is. I said information that could be used, I didn't say used successfully."

"But you're in Daytona, not Jacksonville or Orlando. Are you targeting the St. John's Clinic?"

"I'm making discreet inquiries. I could walk in and say hello. I'm affiliated with Blue Ridge, and clinics do exchange legitimate information. Some of our scientists know their colleagues at St. John's informally. I'd probably be given the grand tour, but I'm not ready for that yet."

"Anything specific taken or just random research information?"

She climbed out of the cart and pulled her driver from the bag. "Among other items, we believe all our data on pyrogia was illegally downloaded."

"Pyrogia?"

"Rare genetic disease that causes aging. Or it did before we cured it. A six-year-old child with pyrogia looked like he was sixty, a seven-year-old looked seventy. By nine they died of old age. Very rare but very deadly. Scientists identified it during the last century, but we couldn't cure it until recently. In our research, we've made discoveries about growth processes and the genetics of the disease."

"Fascinating. When did the theft occur?"

"We discovered it relatively recently. However, we suspect the medical espionage may have been going on for years before we plugged the leak."

"Someone under suspicion?"

"One of our researchers is on administrative leave, but we can't prove anything yet."

"And Cheruba?"

"He does his thing. I do mine. We know one another."

I wasn't satisfied with that answer, but I let it drop.

"How long would it take to build a Jackal?"

"Honey, since no one's ever done it, I have no idea," she told me.

"Thanks for sharing."

She smiled. "As payment, give me a rendition of 'Walking to New Orleans.' Your singing is almost as good as your golf."

After the eighteenth hole, I showered. I stood under the hot spray and thought about what Sierra had said. Sometimes, at least with me, a eureka moment can hit in the shower; a good idea, a connection between two events not previously noticed, a solution to a nagging problem with the golf swing.

But nothing today. Nothing except a whisper of a thought that I was missing something. An obvious clue that I had overlooked. Perhaps my emotions clouded my mind. I had seen Sierra's sharp, look of concern when I mentioned Cheruba. The two did not just have a professional relationship. I felt the jagged ache of regret. *But it was never to be anyway,* I told myself, *so don't let it cloud your judgment.* But what was Cheruba doing here? Was he the Liquidator that took out Meeks? If so, why stick around? What were the chances of two professional Liquidators traveling to Daytona Beach? But if I were a true professional, I would stay undercover. Let attention be focused on Cheruba and, yes, on Drake and keep to the shadows. Do your job and leave before anyone is the wiser.

I dried off and walked to my locker, nodding to the silent Guardian as I went. You don't have to worry about thefts any more. Or someone going through your pockets. Guardians know who is who and what locker they're supposed to be at. They're silent and unobtrusive until something goes wrong. Of course, nothing had gone wrong in years, perhaps decades. You don't mess with a Guardian.

I slipped on some green slacks, a yellow golf shirt, and walked into the lounge. Jan Lakely, a tall, attractive woman, sat at a table before the large picture window. Behind her two golfers stood at the first tee. One grabbed his club and walked between the blue markers. Jan frowned and chewed on a toothpick. Usually, she flashes a car-headlight, wide-beamed smile. Today, she frowned. A waiter took her an iced tea. She picked it and took a quick sip.

I walked over and said hi. I thought she might wave me off, but her fingers pointed toward the chair on the other side of the table. She picked up another toothpick and stuck it between her teeth.

"It's a sunny day, Jan, but you look cloudy."

She nodded. The toothpick had a tiny green ribbon at the tip. She tapped in on the white tablecloth. "I don't know when to keep my big mouth shut."

"Tell a potential buyer a house was termite infested?"

"Ha! I wish." She threw her head back and chuckled. "I wish it were that simple."

I signaled to the waiter. He knew my order.

"Want to talk about it?"

She took another swig of her tea. "Might as well. It can't hurt and it might make be feel better. It's about Garrick."

"I can't see you two having marital problems."

She shook her head. "We're not. It's not that. In fact—" she pointed her finger at me—"do you know I have one of the finest husbands in the world? The man even teaches Sunday School!"

"Yep."

"Do you know the line that perfectly describes Garrick?"

"Well, I have a limited knowledge of Scripture, but I can take a guess. The one where Jesus is describing Philip. 'Behold an Israelite in whom there is no guile,' " I said.

"Absolutely. No guile. No deception. No dishonesty. No games."

"It's wonderful we still have such people."

"Yes, well his wonderful traits are not shared by his siblings. A brother and sister. Sister Vera lives up in Georgia. Brother Todd up in North Carolina. Never liked either of them, with good reason." She picked up her glass and swirled the drink. "Garrick has no guile. They have no honesty." She pointed her finger at me again. "People can take advantage of those with no guile. Siblings can take advantage of them."

I nodded. "That's why it's good he married you. You are not quite as trusting as Garrick. The con men can't get through you."

She leaned back and looked toward the first tee. "You know what got me irritated?"

"No."

"His brother and sister have always resented Garrick. I don't know why, but they have. Even today, I don't think he realizes that. The only time his brother calls is to ask for money. Garrick didn't realize that either. He often calls his siblings, just to say hello or see how they are. Garrick is a great people person. Sold insurance, worked his way up to vice-president of the company. Great salary, and we made wise investments. I contribute with the part-time real-estate income, but we worked for it. Nothing was given to us."

I nodded.

"Last week we had a disagreement. You don't fight with my husband; you only have disagreements. I told him his brother only talks to us when he wants money. Garrick disagreed, saying he and Todd talk a lot. I said you talk about family when you call him. When he calls you, he wants money, and that's the only time he calls. The disagreement was still in the air yesterday when Todd calls. So Garrick is talking and smiling at me in a 'see-you-were-wrong' look. I just wait. So after about five minutes, Todd hits us up for money. He says he had a business setback. Garrick's face falls. He realizes I was right. Todd doesn't care if Garrick lives or dies, but it's good to have a brother around when you need a loan. Loan, my foot—it's a gift. This is not the first time he has asked for funds, and it won't be the last. Garrick agrees to give Todd some money of course, money that we will never see again. If Garrick were Catholic, he'd be up for sainthood, but he is hurt. I can tell."

"Maybe it's good for him to know."

"I dunno." She took another sip of her tea. "Garrick truly believed they were a close family, held together by bonds of affection and blood. Yet if his brother and sister don't need money for the rest of their lives, we will never hear from them again. Which wouldn't bother me, but it does unsettle Garrick."

I thanked the waiter when he set my drink down.

"Again, Jan. That's an unpleasant fact of life, but it is a fact. It's probably better for Garrick to realize that than to..."

She shook her head. "I'm not sure. What would it have mattered if Garrick lived a full life, died, and—as we say in the church—went home to be with the Lord at a ripe old age, still thinking his siblings loved him? Did this unpleasant fact need to be revealed?" She stuck her finger in the air again. "You know what else bothers me?"

I shook my head.

"I am satisfied with my life. Satisfied, hey, I'm downright overjoyed. I love my husband. Jeff and Donne are in Little League and I cheer them on. Jeff plays second base and Donne is in left field. Both are good fielders and pretty good hitters. I love watching them play. My darling Tiffy is six and is the apple not only of her father's eye but is beloved by her brothers too. I've seen little sibling rilvary."

"That's wonderful. Sometimes even siblings get along,"

"In other words, I enjoy each day. So why should I get so upset with Todd and his feckless sister? She's six hundred miles away, and he's even farther up the road."

"For one reason, you may not like seeing Garrick taken advantage of."

She shrugged. "Nah. I think I just didn't want him to make their lives any easier. I never liked either of them and don't understand why they regard Garrick with disdain. Some people simply hate goodness, and innocence. They try to corrupt it or take advantage of it. Garrick has a shrewd business mind, but, in many ways, is an innocent."

"Which is why he needs you around."

She drained her tea and placed it on a tray when the waiter came by. She ordered another, sighed deeply, then looked my way. "Thank you for listening to my rant. Care to vent back?

I'm good for at least thirty minutes."

"No, but there is something you can tell me."

"Name it."

"Merrill Meeks. Didn't you have some dealings with him? Like to know your impression."

She raised her eyebrows. "Is this random curiosity? Or is it professional?"

"The latter."

"I've had some dealings with him, particularly when he was developing Island Shores, which turned out to be one of his major successes. Don't let the rural country boy act fool you. Merrill can be vulgar. In fact, sometimes he delights in it. But dress him in a coat and tie and take that cigar away from him and he can be puppy-dog enthusiastic about a project. His dynamism can spark up your energy too. When he wants something he can oil you like those beach sun bunnies spraying on lotion. He'll bask and butter you like a Thanksgiving turkey. But when you are no more use to him, he'll cut your legs off. He can look and sound swamp-crude, but he has a clever mind. He looks ahead. Most people said Island Shores would flop, but it's a haven of the rich now. He can spot trends, and not just in business. When he wants to, he can digest grade-A science texts. His scientists at the St. John's Clinic know more than he does, but he can ask intelligent questions."

"Was Wes much like him?"

She shook her head. "Only in temperament. He was third-rate Merrill. Didn't have any of the cunning or savvy of his father. Without a rich daddy, he would have landed in prison."

My finger pointed toward the picture window and the first tee. "That little atomic disaster of ten, twelve years ago. Did Merrill have anything to do with that?"

"Nope. That's the one thing you can't pin on him. What was the company's name? Daytona Atomic? Something like that. Merrill did own a small part of the firm at one time but he had sold it before they set up shop here."

I nodded. About ten miles inland the state had placed a toxic waste dump. About fifteen years ago, Daytona Atomic opened a small nuclear research facility next to it. In theory, it was perfectly safe, but theories have a way of being different than reality. Three years after it opened, an atomic accident occurred. Radioactive matter spilled into the atmosphere. The county and state responded, and all the high-tech equipment kept the accident contained. But about five square miles remained radioactive. If you stay inside for several hours, radiation sickness will hit you, not that there was anything worth seeing, or doing, inside. The whole area had been closed off. The state kept a small office on the outskirts to monitor the site and to ensure no random hunter wandered in on the wrong trail.

Jan raised her glass. "I'm glad Wes is dead. We really shouldn't have allowed Merrill to reproduce."

"Why did he establish St. John's? I don't see Merrill acting altruistically."

The green ribbon jerked up and down as Jan chewed on the toothpick.

"That puzzled a lot of people. Before that, Merrill had not shown much curiosity about science. He had fingers in a lot of pies but they were all businesses, and different type of investments. Most of his investments paid off." She shrugged. "It might be he was getting old and wanted to be remembered for something more than making money. He was also concerned with the Meeks' name and the Meeks' legacy. He wanted a son long before he had Wes. He might have set up the clinic to help humanity.

"If he wanted to help humanity, he wouldn't have had Wes."

Jan snickered. "We go to church almost every Sunday. So officially I believe everyone can be redeemed and that no one is out of the reach of God's love." She raised her glass. "Unofficially, we owe a debt of gratitude to the Liquidator."

We clicked our glasses.

As I stood up to go, Jan ordered a sandwich. I waved goodbye. She smiled.

At the door I looked back. Jan stared out toward the green fairway. Beneath her superficial toughness was gentleness and love. Beneath Garrick's innocence was toughness and integrity. In his job, he had faced a number of difficult decisions. He had always come down on the side of honesty, even when tempted to shade the figures. The two had found one another.

Life always does its best to break you. Sometimes it fails, and a few couples find happiness.

Sanchez didn't waste time. The Courier waited patiently by my office door. His eyes flashed green as a signal. Couriers are supposed to look human so they can walk undetected among crowds. This one appeared as a stout, balding man with a harmless grin. His red and green beach shirt was crowded with palm trees and fruit drinks.

"Come in. We can talk in my office," I said.

"Mind if I do a retina scan first?"

"Be my guest."

His eyes didn't light up this time, but a slight warmth ran across mine. I opened the door and we walked in. He stood in the middle of the room.

"My client extends his apologies. He did not realize you were in this area nor did he think his actions would cause you harm or even concern," the Courier said.

"What's your name?"

"Mac."

Words flowed gently from Mac. No tinny, metallic voice, rather a soft, melodic tenor of a beloved grandfather. He should have been in the diplomatic core.

"Mac, did your client happen to steer the Meeks family in my direction?"

"No. He asked me to reassure you that he said nothing and did nothing that would lead anyone to suspect you. He believes that your prior experience with Merrill Meeks caused him to suspect you. As noted, he did not realize you were in the area. He was brought in from the North. It is unfortunate that you are involved. If he could undo the situation and give you warning, he would."

"And when he hooked Meeks up to the TC computer, what did he find out?"

Mac didn't change his tone or his smile. He remained the genial, balding stranger bearing bad news. "My client regrets he cannot reveal that information."

"Why not?"

"He did not tell me why. He only said it would be impossible to comply with your request at this time. When it becomes possible, he will send another message and answer your question."

I put my hands on my coat, brushing back my coat to reveal my shoulder holster and gun. "Well, that was a lot of help."

Mac nodded. "I'm glad."

Sierra was right. Robots can't think, and neither do they have an appreciation of sarcasm.

"Is that your entire message?"

"Yes, and that my client wishes you well."

"Nice of him."

Mac bowed slightly and slipped out the door.

I chewed on my lower lip, revealing my annoyance. The Liquidator should have been back above the Mason-Dixon line. There was at least one reason why he couldn't reveal the information I wanted. He was still in town and had other work to do. Meeks' answers related to the Liquidator's next target. But who?

Eleven

New Orleans, 1846

Customers eyed the duo that entered the Delta Queen, one of the finest restaurants in the city. To a casual observer, the tall man and dark-haired woman looked no different than the three dozen other elegantly dressed couples. Eight couples danced. Others sat at tables. The waiters busily brought food and drink. The gaslight lamps on the walls bathed the room in a soft, gold light. Two candles were on each table. After giving his silver-tipped cane and hat to the steward, the tall man escorted the lady to a large table, decorated with a gold and white tablecloth. The gold-rimmed plates and silverware reflected the glare of the candlelight. The gentleman moved a chair back for the lady, who thanked him as she sat down. A waiter did the same for him.

It was rumored the tall gentleman in the burgundy waistcoat and white silk shirt was a merchant from Florida who had recently moved to the Crescent City, although few things were known about his background. But he had been readily accepted into the social life of the city. It was rumored he may have had some royalty in his background, a vague but nonetheless legitimate ancestor to French counts and barons. Many residents of New Orleans had fled the French Revolution and had had relatives or friends executed, so the possible royal lineage was a high mark in the man's favor. Slightly pale, there was no Spanish or creole blood in the man and he was taller than most other men in the room. At least six-three. In 1846 New Orleans, most men were medium-height.

His escort was the daughter of the Telmunds, a prominent family of New Orleans. Well-educated, she spoke three languages and was stunning in the blue dress, cut just low enough on her neck to be noticeable, without being scandalous. If not distracted by her beauty, most men—and certainly most women—would be distracted by the glamorous white diamond necklace on her slender neck, offset by the shining white gloves.

They moved onto the dance floor and flowed easily with the other couples as swirled around the room. Both the man and the woman moved fluidly and gracefully. The man smiled but looked content and at ease in the room, as if he had been there before which, of course, he had. The lady, though, while bedazzling the room with her smile, looked equally bedazzled, an expression of awe on her young face, A few times she seemed breathless, and put a white-gloved hand across her heart. At such a young age, she was not fatigued, but overwhelmed by the magnificence of the room and the assorted couples.

As they twirled on the dancefloor, suddenly the gentleman began singing a love song. Surprisingly, several other gentleman joined in with perfect harmony. The lady, stunned at first, almost fainted with delight. Her companion continued the serenade while they danced, swirling around from one end of the floor to the other. When the music ended, the lady smiled with great delight and managed a brief bow, as did the other ladies on the dance floor. The gentlemen responded.

As it sensing she was overwhelmed, the gentleman took her hand and walked her back to their table, again pulling out her chair, which is something men did in 1846 in old New Orleans.

There was no casual observer in the room, but if there had been, he would have noticed that the conversation of the merchant and the Telmunds' daughter was not similar to the conversations of the other couples. The latter talked about business or family matters or politics or perhaps the arts. Two talked of an astonishing twelve-year-old chess player from a local family who had bested several accomplished, much older players. The Florida gentleman and his companion spoke of other things.

All talk was silenced when three other gentleman approached the couple's table. One carried a burnished dark wood case. The man in the middle was only five-five and of moderate built, with blond hair but of darker skin than the man from Florida. He seemed to command the men with him. A priest rushed over and spoke, but the blond man, in a polite, almost apologetic manner, waved him aside. The priest refused to move.

The Florida merchant stood up as the men approached. The blond man first apologized to the lady for the interruption. She nodded gracefully. He replied with a polite bow before addressing her companion. A certain Andrew Duplantis had died suddenly and this was the same man who was scheduled to meet him on the field of honor, after slandering him. Now the honor passed to his second.

"You have your choice of weapons," the blond man said.

The dark wood case was opened to show two silver dueling pistols.

"Or swords if you prefer," the man added.

"Swords are my first choice," came the answer from the Florida merchant.

"And your name, sir?" the blond man asked.

When the name was announced, a second hush fell over the room. Not everyone on the dance floor or at the tables recognized the stranger but, even in his short time in New Orleans, Jefferson Drake had established a reputation as a excellent swordsman. The blond gentleman was known to be skilled with swords but did not have the ability of a Jefferson Drake. Duels were fought at dawn. Most of the men and women in the room realized, on the day of the duel, the blond man would be dead a few minutes after the sun rose.

The blond man shook his head, as if slapped. He was stunned by the disclosure, but could not back down. He stammered, but the Florida merchant raised his hand.

Then came what all agreed was an eloquent speech and a magnificent gesture by the stranger. He began by saying Andrew Duplantis was a long-time friend who had even saved his life, and that he would always be loyal to him. But his friend had a great flaw. In James, the apostle says we must learn to control our tongue. As some men can never control their intake of whisky and others cannot control their gambling, Drake admitted his friend could not control his tongue. He made statements that were not only ungracious and inappropriate for polite society, but also untrue. Drake told the blond man that whatever statement his friend had made was not true and offered an apology.

"Andrew was forever my friend," the Florida merchant said, "but I cannot excuse or justify his sin. Nor do I wish to kill a man because of his recklessness or, for that matter, be killed due to it. If this apology is sufficient, please accept it. If not, then I am bound to meet you on the field of honor."

Before the blond man could answer, the priest spoke hastily and urged him to accept. There was no need for bloodshed, he said.

In fact the blond gentleman looked much relieved and said no duel would be necessary and expressed thanks for the apology.

"Also, most duels take place at dawn, and I regret to say I am not a morning person, so I try to avoid them whenever possible," Drake said, to much laughter in the room.

Even the blond gentleman threw back his head and

laughed. Then Drake called for the steward and asked that the best wine in the restaurant be delivered to the blond gentleman's table, a gesture the crowd clearly appreciated.

He sat down and smiled at his companion. "I thought a little theatre would enliven the evening, but I assumed you would not want to see an actual duel."

"That's correct," Lori said. "But you did not have to enliven the evening. It has been spectacular."

Drake lifted his glasss. Lori smiled and lifted her coffee cup.

"To the beauty of New Orleans, which almost matches the beauty of my companion."

"Thank you, sir," Lori said. "Have you come here often?"

"Not often. Occasionally. Sometimes you want to get away and a different time and a different place look inviting, at least for a while. You can become another person, with another name but write your own background. To the others in the room we are Jefferson Drake and Katherine Telmund."

Lori smiled. "I appreciate it, but I've never wanted to be anyone else. I'm glad about who I am. But I do like good restaurants, in any time period."

"OK. Where would you like to go next?"

"Oh! Antoine's. Can we go to Antoine's next?"

"Certainly. You've heard of Antoine's?"

"Yes, it's one of the most famous restaurants in the world."

"Any particular time period."

"Contemporary."

"I'll make the arrangements."

She set her cup down. "The coffee is real."

He nodded. "Yes."

"But the room isn't, not really."

"The room is real. Most of the images are artificial, but the waiters are real. The food is real. And I'm guessing one or two other couples are real and also wanted dinner out. It is truly an evening in New Orleans in 1846. This club has the finest holographic technology in the South. Name a period and place, and you get historical accuracy down to the fine linen."

"Almost. Did they sing in old New Orleans?"

He smiled. "Well, a few things are added."

Lori looked around. "Do some people...get lost in here?"

"In here? No, the club doesn't allow it. In holographic space? Yes. Some people get lost and don't ever quite find their way back."

Lori sipped her coffee, then swirled the liquid in her cup as she surveyed the room. Her glance swept past her companion to the artificial restaurant.

"Has something upset you?" he asked.

"I was wondering about those men who prefer holograms to reality...and do they prefer holographic women to humans."

Drake nodded. "Some do. You can have Helen of Troy, the Queen of Sheba, or your pick of movie stars at your fingertips. Human women have their own minds, their own emotions, and might say no. Why bother with them?"

"Why indeed," Lori said.

After dinner, we had another turn on the dance floor and Lori impressed the artificial crowd with her gracefulness. I held her hand as we returned to our seats. She smiled, but the earlier vitality wasn't there.

As I pushed her chair in, I asked, "Is something troubling you?"

She dipped a spoon filled with a dollop of sugar into her coffee and stirred the liquid. "I don't want to spoil the evening."

"No, tell me. What's wrong."

She leaned back and sipped the coffee. "I don't know. I just don't like being in an artificial setting. This is not real and, for some reason, it bothers me, although New Orleans in 1846 is a romantic place to be."

"Apparantly, not romantic enough."

"It's not you, Jerico. I love your company." She shook her head. "I'm just not comfortable. This is false, it's phony."

"It's real to some people."

"Not to me."

I reached out and touched her hand. "Maybe it's because you're a Christian. You believe in truth, so you're upset by this fake setting. It's nice, but it's not 'truth.'"

"Perhaps. My spirit is troubled. Don't you believe in truth?"

"I lean that way." I shrugged. "Next time we could program in the crucifixion or the resurrection. I hear those are two popular topics too."

"No!"

Her sharp tone startled me.

"That would be phony too. The sacrifice of Jesus was not fake. It's real. He died so we might live forever. He gave himself to redeem the human race. An artificial setting wouldn't bring you closer to him. I've read the accounts of the crucifixion, prayed, and meditated about them. I've seen it in my spirit. There's nothing holograms could add."

"Sorry, I didn't mean to upset you."

"That's all right. But let's change the subject and talk about something real." She gestured toward me with the white-gloved hand. "The psychological profile of Merrill Meeks."

"That's not just real, that's depressing," I said. "Although I did want any insights you might have. Do you agree with my hunch?"

She moved forward and placed her elbows on the table. "I do. I've read everything on the Internet about Meeks and listened as you described him. You were wondering, if he did hire an assassin, would he want the—" she gulped—"the murder carried out quickly, hit-and-run so to speak, or would he want something more personal?"

I nodded. "That question had crossed my mind."

"This is diagnosis by distance since I haven't talked to him, but I would say Meeks would not want his Jackal, or whatever it is he has created, to kill you from a distance. The death of his son is very personal. I'm guessing he would want the Jackal to get the drop on you, then tell you who sent him and why. The Jackal would then report back to his boss and Meeks would enjoy hearing how he killed you. No doubt the Jackal is equipped with a camera. Meeks could view your demise time and time again." She looked uncomfortable again, shifting in her seat. Finally, she spoke. "I'm guessing Meeks would not..."

"Would not want me killed too quickly," I said.

She said nothing but nodded.

That confirmed my own hunch about Meeks. He wouldn't want a sniper as an assassin. He'd want it close up.

"Jerico, he is an evil man. Shouldn't you go to the police?"

"With only a rumor? No. But I know how to take care of myself."

I was surprised, and delighted, when her gloved fingers brushed my cheek. The lamps burned brighter when she smiled.

"I hope so. I'm praying for you."

The affection in her voice changed the universe from something alien and ugly to something beautiful.

Twelve

The house alarm flared at 3 a.m. Two seconds later, my feet hit the cold floor and my gun pointed at the outside darkness. I eased into shoes and slipped on a jacket over the sweatpants. I walked to the small room where the security system's screens hummed and blinked. The mile radius of my house was clear. No threatening red dots moved toward the house. Francine doesn't wake me when small animals scurry among beach hedges. Her sensors are also keen enough to detect that random drunks are, in fact, intoxicated and are no threat, particularly if they're not armed. The lasers stay on stun.

"What's happening, Francine?"

There was a pause before she replied. "I don't quite know, Jerico."

Not a reply you want from a security computer.

"Was there an intruder?"

"Yes, on the perimeter. Just inside of the mile radius."

"Human?"

There was another pause. That's unusual for a computer.

"Perhaps."

"Perhaps? Was it a robot?"

"Possible."

"Wait a minute. Was the intruder a human or a robot?"

"It was both, and neither."

I laid the gun on a counter. "Thanks. That clears it up." I looked at the screen. "I assume whatever it was is gone now."

"Yes."

"Francine. Upgrade the lasers. Put them on kill." I walked to a window, pulled back the drapes, and peered out into the blackness. "Francine, your lasers can kill a human. Could they stop a robot?"

"Yes."

"Even if one had, say, reenforced armor?"

"I could burn a hole in it, Jerico."

I smiled. "That's comforting."

Even so, New Orleans in 1846 was looking better all the time.

* * *

Duffy Robeson had left a message on my answering machine. He wanted to meet at the Daytona Sunset bar around three. Robeson often did freelance work for detective agencies, defense attorneys, bail bondsmen, or random millionaires. We had always gotten along well. I had put out feelers, and wondered if Robeson had any worthwhile information.

Some delirious interior decorator had decked out the Dayton Sunset almost entirely in red. Red tablecloths, red chairs, red foam at the bar. The waitresses wore black and white uniforms though, with the black skirt ending just about three inches below their hips I settled comfortably at a table, ordered a drink, and waited for Duffy. He's a friendly, smiling man with an easy charm and a gambler's manner. Although not in a stress-free job, he's a pharmaceutical company's nightmare. He takes tranquilizers as often as a Pentecostalist drinks whisky. A cat looks tense besides Duffy.

He slid into the opposite booth a few minutes later, giving me a warm greeting and a big smile. His granite features are made softer by his amiable personality and wide grin. He ordered a drink and, when the waitress turned to go back to the bar, he winked and smiled.

"Jenny just had a bad breakup. Need to give her encouragement," he said. "Wonderful gal."

"I'll leave a big tip. That should help too."

He edged forward. "I'm been informed of your problem, Jerico. Naturally, I'd like to help. I have some information that may put an entirely different prospective on your situation."

"I hope it's a better prospective."

"That I don't know. It's more puzzling, if this is true."

He paused as the encouraged waitress, a slender blond with startling gray eyes, placed Duffy's drink before him. He patted her hand this time. "Jerico's a friend and he tips well. But we won't need any more unless we signal you, honey."

"OK, Duffy."

He sipped his Scotch and soda. "What would you say if I told you Wes Meeks might be alive?"

"I'd say that's impossible, unless they ran off copies of him."

I lit a cigar as Duffy polished off his drink. He scratched his neck.

"This is going to sound odd, but bear with me. Do you remember the Wikiki Club?"

"The strip joint? Excuse me—'adult entertainment establishment'?"

"That's the one. About six, seven years ago we were working a case together and shadowing a guy who went in for a show. Remember Cherry Delight?"

"Ah, yes. The dancer who wore fake, artificial cherries but would peel them off during her show and toss them to the audience."

"That's the one. If you were lucky, you'd get a souvenir of her dance."

I smiled. "She was memorable."

"Well, after nine or ten years at the club, Peggy—that's her real name—is retiring. She made out real well and bought a thirty-acre spread in Jackson County over in the Panhandle. Wouldn't have thought Peggy was a country girl, would you? Turns out she loves horses and wide open spaces. Told me she was never going near a club again. On her good months, and on my good months, she'd got a couple of thousand of my money alone. Anyway, I was at one of her last performances. It was Cherry at her best. She was swinging and pivoting to the music, driving all the customers wild. Cherries flew all over the place." He pointed a finger at me. "I swear to you, Jerico, I saw Wesley M. Meeks at the show."

"*The* Wesley Meeks? The *dead* Wesley Meeks?"

Robeson nodded. "He had this dumb wig, straight black hair, and a fake mustache, but it was Meeks. I know the guy. He was a regular. He'd been going there for four, five years, ever since he could legally get through the Guardians. That stunned me, so after the show I go back and see Peggy and ask her about it. She said it looked like Meeks. The guy had, as she put it, 'those same psycho eyes' as Meeks had. She admitted she didn't get a real close look, but the guy make her skin crawl, just like Meeks."

I sighed and blew out some smoke. "It has to be a second cousin, or someone else who looks like him. The dead body of Wes Meeks was identified in any number of ways, including DNA analysis, fingerprints, and retina scan."

Robeson swirled the drink in his glass, then drank it down. "Maybe, but look at it this way. Suppose, just suppose, if Meeks were alive, he'd know a Liquidator is on his trail, plus a few other people who wouldn't mind taking a shot at him. He'd have to lay low. But he's been a steady customer at the Wikiki, and Cherry was his favorite dancer. It would be like him—in spite of the danger—to see her one last time and drop in during her final week. He was the customer who flopped two thousand dollar bills down and told Cherry and Orange—"

"Orange?"

"Orange Blossom. She's another dancer there...came in about three years ago."

Many things change as the centuries roll on. The sole exception may be the names of strippers.

"Anyway, he flipped the bills on the table and Orange and Cherry grabbed them as fast as he handed them out, then gave him a kiss. You know the rules. No hands at the club, but the dancers are allowed to give a little peck on the cheek. Another time he told the fruity two he had a load of hundreds for them if they only had something to carry the dollars in. A Texas gentleman who happened to be visiting said, "Allow me, darlings," and laid out the biggest handkerchief you'd ever seen. They scooped the money up and scampered off. Meeks was one of the more avid customers of the club...more like addicted, really. He would want one last look."

I chewed on my cigar. "If anything could bring you back from the dead, a Cherry dance could do it."

"Well, I just wanted to let you know."

"I appreciate that."

I deposited the cigar in an ashtray. I was beginning to have doubts. Doubts about everything.

"Duffy, about the guy in the wig. How sure are you? Could it really have been Meeks?"

"If you hooked me up to a TC computer and asked if I had seen Wes Meeks, I'd say yes and the computer would hum. No loud noises."

I kept my promise and left a big tip. On any other day I would have noticed the bright sunshine. Such a yellow day makes you smile, lifts depression, and starts you thinking toward beaches, bikinis, and golf. But there was a fog around me.

Duffy is reliable and dependable, and rarely mistaken. But the dead do not return for a second chance, not even for one last look at the enchanting Cherry Delight.

So what is going on?

Ben Adonal stood between first and second base, the brown infield sand beneath his feet. In back of him, the green grass of the outfield sprang up. His oldest child was only six, too young for Little League, but Ben served as an umpire due to sheer love of the game. He usually worked with Terry Freniere. The chemistry was right although, on the surface, they were nothing alike. As an assistant state attorney and upright straight-arrow, Ben always looked like a Sunday School teacher, hair-in-place, immaculate shirt and pants. Freniere carried about fifty extra pounds, was twenty years older than Ben, slovenly, and had a black and gray ponytail that hung halfway to his waist. Freniere was careless about dress but precise when it came to calling strikes and balls. He was a great umpire. Freniere was usually behind the plate while Ben handled the base paths.

I munched on some popcorn while Ben called an out at first base. I waited patiently while the Marauders squeezed out an 8-6 win over the Hilltoppers, a mild upset since the latter team held first place in the league.

After the players cleared the field, Ben walked over to the bleachers and sat down beside me.

"What can I do for you, Jerico? You like baseball, but I figured you didn't come out here just to watch the game."

"No, but I think the Marauders' right fielder has talent."

"Yes, he does."

"Speaking of talent in a different area, your office tries to keep track of Liquidators, right?"

"We try."

"So are any in the area?"

"Besides Cheruba?"

"Yes. Besides Cheruba. I'm impressed. Your office seems to be first-rate."

"He flew in a couple of weeks ago. We keep an eye on him, but it's not a twenty-hour watch. He spends most of his time on the beach."

"Anyone else?"

He shook his head. "Not to my knowledge. But that doesn't mean there isn't one. It simply means we don't know about him."

I grunted. "I have information that the Liquidator who killed Meeks is still in town too."

Ben paused. "That would be unusual. Do you know that for sure? Firsthand information?"

"No. Let's just say it's an educated guess."

"Why would the Liquidator stick around?"

"That's the question I asked myself."

"Did you come up with an answer?"

"The only thing I can think of is he has other business here."

"Do Liquidators give discounts now?" Ben asked. "A two for one deal?"

"I don't think so."

"Meeks the wrong target?"

"I doubt that too. Which means I have no idea of what's going on." I turned to him and smiled. "So I thought I would ask a professional."

Ben thought for a moment. "I can't help you much. Most of what we know about the Meeks' case is already public information. Whatever is secret, I can't divulge, even to you, Jerico."

"I realize that. But I'm wondering if a second Liquidator had been visiting the tourist sites."

"Not to our knowledge." Ben paused again. "But I can tell

you something we found puzzling."

"By all means."

"Carter Dunlop has been hanging around Merrill Meeks a lot lately. He's been out to the St. John's clinic a couple of times, although he's never been known to be an avid science buff."

"I wonder what type of business Meeks has for him."

Ben looked at me. "Dunlop has been involved in a lot of criminal activities. He's served a couple of years for assault and robbery convictions, but I've never known him to kill for hire. But, as I mentioned to you, he's in some financial trouble."

"Merrill could certainly get him out of it. But I've also heard Merrill is building a Jackal."

Ben shook his head. "An artificial hit man is all we need. We have enough trouble with flesh-and-blood murderers." He glared at me. "Not that I believe it. It's never been done, so we can't give those rumors much credibility."

I finished off the popcorn, wadded up the bag, and tossed it into a container. "Thanks for the information."

"Keep in touch," Ben said as I walked away.

I had slid into the driver's seat when I remember there was one question I had forgotten to ask Ben. Actually, not forgotten. I just hesitated to ask Ben if he was sure Wes Meeks was actually dead. In the cold light of day, it seemed like a stupid question. Then again...I looked at the bleachers, but Ben had already slipped away.

It could wait for another time. Maybe at the next game.

Thirteen

The Driftwood restaurant was as clean and as scenic as it had been the last time Mullet and I lunched. We had a beachside table. Mullet smiled when the waiter placed the huge bowl of clam chowder in front of him. His aim was better this time. Almost all the pepper flakes dropped into the creamy chowder. Mullett stirred it, then lifted a spoonful to his mouth. He gulped it down and sighed. "Best chowder on the coast. Wish I could eat here every day."

I handed him the envelope of money. "This should help with a few dinners."

Mullet took the envelope and deposited it in his shirt pocket. He didn't bother to count it. Either he was getting senile, or he was too hungry to bother. Or he trusted me. But Mullet was steak-knife sharp mentally, and didn't trust anyone. So he was hungry.

He patted his coat pocket. "I appreciate it, buddy. Times have been thin lately."

"And the information you have is..."

He smiled. "You got a few more days. The Jackal isn't ready."

"So I have time to make out my will."

"I wouldn't joke about this, Jerico. Merrill Meeks is dead serious."

"No pun intended, I assume."

Mullet frowned, then shrugged. "They tested it, but there were some malfunctions. So it went back to the lab.

Technicians are hovering over it now. It will have only one command." Mullet pointed his spoon at me. "Kill Jerico Drake."

"I'm such a sweet guy too."

"Not to Meeks. He hates you. He hated you even before you killed Wes."

"Mullet, I didn't kill Wes."

He waved away my objections with his spoon, flicking a bit of chowder in the wind. "Whatever you say. You won three hundred thousand from him one night. It's not like he'd miss it, but he hates to lose."

I nodded. "After that, he stopped coming to the club, at least for poker nights. Or at least he stopped playing with me, although I'd assumed he would want a chance to win his money back."

"He's got a better way of revenge. By the way, what were you playing?"

"Five card. I got lucky."

He swallowed another spoonful of chowder. A thin white line ran down his chin. He wiped it away with a blue napkin. "Heard he had three Queens."

"I had three Jacks."

"So how did you—"

"And two sevens."

Mullet's low whistle rippled the surface of the chower. "One heck of a good hand for five card. No wonder Merrill is in a blue funk."

"I was going for other colors, but he quit coming. So when do they expect the Jackal will be ready?"

"Couple of days. Maybe a week."

I leaned across the table and lowered my voice, although there was no one around us. All other customers were seated inside, away from the Florida sun. Mullet serenely crunched crackers.

"Mullet, you mentioned they tested the Jackal and it

malfunctioned. Just when did they test it, and where?"

He shrugged. "Don't know that. I don't have details." He put his spoon down in his chowder and watched it sink into the bowl. His hands sliced the air as he talked. The only way he could sit still was if someone tied him down.

"This thing not only has lethal software and brain cells focused on killing you, they're installing the best defenses. In theory, he can slip through most residential radar screens. Maybe not those on a military base—the army has the ultra-sophisticated stuff—but homes are something else."

Despite the best efforts of Meeks' roboticists, I'd still bet on Francine, although I decided to have her upgraded. Then let the thing try to come to me. I'd be ready. I inched an eyebrow up but kept my voice low. "Mullet, why don't you tell me who you're getting your information from?"

"Jerico, I can't do that. I can't rat somebody out. Besides, isn't it against the law—some type of confidentiality? Husband and wife, doctor and patient."

"You don't fall under any of those categories. My life is at stake here, Mullet, and I want to know how credible your information is."

I got his attention. He stopped eating. He chewed on his lower lip. His spoon clanged against the dish as his hand shook. He looked around nervously.

"Besides Mullet, I carry a gun." I showed him a wide smile.

He swallowed. "OK, but you can't tell anyone."

"Wasn't planning to."

"One of the scientists is talking to me. A Dr. Barlow Maddoz."

"How did you get to know one of Meeks' scientists?"

He dipped his spoon into the chowder again. "Same way you got to know Merrill. Poker. You know Josh Luckett?"

"Don't know him but heard of him."

"Then you know he runs poker games at his apartments. For

low-key players…those who don't like the glitz of the casinos. Just no-nonsense guys who like to play poker."

I nodded. I'd had heard that.

"I go over there about twice a week. Some time ago, Barlow began playing. The only trait he shares with his boss is they both enjoy playing poker. Naturally, we started talking. You got a brief mention in the papers when you nabbed that Lester fellow for murder. When was that? Eight months ago?"

"About that. I helped—"

"When you got headlines I mentioned we were friends. Mentioned you again when Wes Meeks got off. Knew you were upset."

"But why is he talking about a Jackal?"

Mullet sipped his beer. "Bar is a good man. They had him working on legitimate medical stuff for years. He was pulled off to work on a Jackal. Meeks didn't even bother to hide his intentions. Anyone who raised questions was threatened. The others were too scared to do anything. Bar is too frightened to go to the police. He's convinced Meeks will kill him, but he doesn't like what he's doing. It's eating him up."

I sat back in the chair. "Is Barlow a good poker player?"

"Fair to middling. He wins some, loses others."

"Does he bluff well?"

"Not particularly. I can usually read him."

"Is he bluffing now?"

Mullet eased the spoon of out the bowl, swallowed the chowder, then shrugged. "I don't think so. I can't think of any reason why he would."

Neither could I.

"I can read people, Jerico, and not just at a poker table. Something is gnawing at him. His game has been off recently and he's been drinking more. He's tense and agitated. If you ask me, I'd say no, he's not bluffing, and he's not lying. And they're almost finished with the Jackal."

Mullet's spoon dipped into the chowder again. "What are they building it with? What material?" I said.

Mullet shook his head. "I don't know. What am I? A metallurgist? It's a robot."

"How strong is the material? Will a bullet from a small handgun penetrate it? Or do I need a .44 magnum?"

"Oh, I see....lemme think. Trying to remember what Bar said.... No specifics, but I know he said they were building it better and stronger than any other robot. It will be stronger than a Guardian. A single bullet won't do much, except maybe blow off a finger. It wouldn't penetrate the thing's chest. And if you're close enough to shoot a finger off, you'll be dead in few seconds."

"But it's back in the shop?"

He nodded. "Maybe a week. They want to be extra cautious. They don't want it to malfunction after they turn it loose. But someone is following you."

I edged closer to him. "You sure? I haven't noticed anyone."

"It's off and on. They figured they don't need to watch you twenty-four hours a day. They know where you are, and they know you're not going anywhere."

I smiled as Lori brought me the cup of Café Caribbean. I sat in an orange chair, smilingly flanked by Duke and Dixie.

"You look concerned, Jerico. What's wrong?"

I sipped the brew and complimented the chef. "Nothing serious. I just recently got a piece of information that was...unexpected."

"About Cary."

"No, about another matter." I shrugged. "But it's probably nothing."

She eased into a chair. "By the way, my computer, Robert, has you in my safe file."

"I thought I was in the sweet and adorable file."

She laughed. "Working up to that. May I ask you something? I thought private detectives worked out of seedy offices, scraped by for a living, and were usually ungrammatical."

"We've moved up in the world, although I am working on my syntax. It's always better to have rich clients. Early in my practice, I had two clients who were large growers and on the Florida Citrus Commission. That's how my name helped me. They had known my father and thought the son of Ben Drake would be the perfect detective for them. I didn't get any inheritance, but the name certainly helped."

Concern dimmed the sparkling eyes. "Your father didn't leave you anything?"

"A small sum. My oldest brother, William, became a lawyer and got a substantial amount. Brother Errol got the real-estate business. He's good in sales. My sister received a house, plus some stock and assets. I got five thousand. I'm not complaining. It was more than I thought I'd get."

She shook her head as if a pail of cold water had been dumped on her. "That's terrible. Didn't you get along with your father?"

"We never had cross words. We just didn't have many words at all."

"Was it because you were genrich?"

I nodded. "That may have been part of it, but it wasn't just with me. My mother favored her oldest. William was always her favorite. I think that hurt Errol more than it did me. William was taller, stronger, more athletic. Errol always fought chubbiness, and was always trying to get Mother's affection but never quite succeeded. I think he's upset by that even today, and is still trying to prove himself. He always wanted to be more athletic than I am, which he isn't, and, now as an adult, wants to make more money than William. He hasn't achieved that fiscal goal either. I think Mother always planned to have three children, but a year or so after Molly was born, having a child that was genrich..."

"Became a status symbol," Lori said.

"Very much so. In her social realm, the women began talking about their children who were genrich, and mother was very conscious of status. So she had another child. But she forgot that her rich friends would talk about the genrich youngest child, and ignore her favored, oldest son. From a very young age I realized I was different, that I was apart from the family group. I never understood why until I got to the age where I understood my genetic status. Very early, Mother begin to resent that I was genrich and William wasn't. She knew I was smarter, quicker, would live longer, and have all the benefits of the genrich. She made sure my siblings knew it too. Errol wanted to curry favor with Mom so he didn't like me either."

"That never changed during your childhood."

I shook my head. "No. The thing is, my brothers are not bad people. I watched with great jealousy when they would laugh and joke with friends. I wanted to be part of their group. I wanted to laugh and joke with them."

She frowned. "Did you ever feel like you were part of a family?"

I realized I wanted something stronger than the Caribbean. "One time. For a few minutes on that day my brothers were true brothers. We had a basketball hoop in the backyard and one day I was playing—alone, of course. Bill walked by with Errol and, for some reason, he decided to join me. Errol followed. For about two hours we were brothers playing basketball: shouting, shooting, competing, encouraging one another. I made one basket and remember Bill yelling, "What a shot!" My sister came out and began cheering, clapping her hands and punching the air. "Go Bill. Make it, Errol. Dunk it, Jerico."

I paused. I remembered the day well. It had become etched in my memory. "For a moment, it seemed as if they had all been playing a role all of my life…the role of indifferent, if not hostile, siblings. But that day on the basketball court, their masks slipped and they forgot to keep acting. They were just two boys and a girl having fun with their brother. I was delighted. That was the happiest time of my childhood."

"How old were you then?"

"About twelve. Molly was fourteen, Errol, I think, was sixteen, and Bill was seventeen. For the first time, there was a bond of friendship and affection between us. But then about six, mom came out in a cold fury. She yelled at us that we shouldn't be playing, that Bill had to be somewhere and Errol was supposed to do this or that. She told Molly she'd be late for some type of practice." I shook my head and gave a wry smile. "You know, I still think she was angry because they were playing with me and I was having fun. Then the masks came back on. I swear I saw—just for a moment —changes in their countenances. The warm, friendly smiles disappeared. The cold indifference was back. They went back in, but I stayed on the court for a moment, silently pleading with them to come back and play."

But they left, and the spectre came in their place, and whispered of death.

"So how did you cope in that situation?"

I shook my head to clear the memories. "I read. Stayed in my room and read. Video games, computers. And sports. I wasn't the only student who joined sporting squads to get away from home. But I genuinely enjoyed baseball and golf. Although in tennis, the girls' team wore real short skirts. All the guys on the golf team tried to get the girls to wear similar short skirts, but they refused."

She sipped her from her cup. "How sad. I can't remember a day when my parents ignored me. They were simply wonderful people. If I stubbed my toe, Mom was there with a Band-Aid. They loved Cary but didn't expect another child, so I was their darling. Didn't get away with a lot, though. Still remember my mother pointing her finger at me and saying, 'Young lady, we do not believe in time-outs in this house. We believe in old-fashioned spankings, and if you ever do that again.... I don't know how I could have survived if that love hadn't been there."

I shrugged. "It's over. It happened when I was a child. No use complaining."

"Some people have the toughest time doing that, which is why I may go into psychology. I already know some genrich kids who may need a little help."

I drained my cup. "Don't hang onto the past, either good or bad. Accept the good times, ignore the bad and go on."

Fourteen

Cary Hallendorf had been a very meticulous man and had remarkably good penmanship. His notes were clear, readable and, I thought, insightful. He had jotted down numerous items via computer but also took copious paper notes. Lines in Munson Cain's books were underlined in red and yellow. A few question marks were scrawled through the type.

After wading through his research for several hours, I came to the conclusion Munson Cain was a repugnant human being, but I had already guessed that. His treatment of his wives was less-than-admirable, to put it mildly. Long-suffering editors took shots of Scotch or heavy doses of tranquilizers after Cain's verbal abuse. When his books were selling, the author would taunt vice-presidents with threats of leaving for other book publishers. When the sales were rolling, no editor wanted to be the man who lost Munson Cain to a competitor.

Yet he had been coasting for decades. None of his novels after *Second-rate Road* were well received. In fact, critics gutted them. But by then Cain was moving into politics as a prominent pseudo-intellectual. Stripped of all the horrific prose, Cain's philosophy seemed to justify criminal action. Hardly new. From time to time, intellectuals have endorsed criminals, becoming backers of cop-killers or other, more ordinary murderers.

Cain seemed to have a degree of luck. His flaws, insecurities, and bluster seem to reflect the temper of the times. His political rants came to the forefront when society was undergoing fundamental changes. Robots were being mass-produced and taking over menial jobs. In the flesh-and-blood realm, genetic engineering was remaking humanity. The genetic technology made many people, including many academics, intellectuals and pundits, uneasy. I wondered if some of the uneasiness was a reflection of ego and pride, not due to any basic concern for society. That elites thought they were better than most of the human race. Many wanted to be leaders, but humanity never bothered to follow them. Some clung to a belief that their intelligence and awareness made them unique and special. Now they were confronting a group of genrich men and women who were vastly superior to the old-guard elite in terms of intelligence and physique. The intellectuals and academics felt embittered and betrayed. Cain fed into that uneasiness and, perhaps, paranoia.

In addition, society had become resegregated. Cain's writing came during the period of tension between radical Muslims and Europeans, the rise of black nationalism, the (unsuccessful) attempt by many of Mexican ancestry to carve out a portion of the southwest and rejoin Mexico, akin to the successful succession of two Canadian provinces from our northern neighbor. Such strife produced a political pot steaming over with anxiety and fear. Cain appealed to many who were both uneasy with their culture and scared due to the political upheavals around them.

Personally, like many rich individuals, Cain had a willing and obedient band of lackeys who followed him around and were verbally and emotionally abused. But the followers had withered like the sales. Hallendorf's wording was precise. I know exactly the outline of his biography. He had scribbled one line in a notebook, and it puzzled me. "Lansdale is the key—the key to everything."

I gave Francine the date of Lansdale's birth and told her to run all information about the man, particularly if he had any living relatives. While she was humming away, I strolled over to the state attorney's office. Ben was preparing for a case so wasn't esctatic about seeing me. I told him I only needed a few minutes.

His desk was as neat as he was. Not a speck of dust. A cockroach wouldn't have dared to crawl across it.

"I can't give out any details about the case," Ben said, in answer to my initial query.

"I don't see how this one fact would hinder any investigation. After all, if you catch the Liquidator, he's probably going to admit guilt and ask the jury to free him. Liquidating a guilty man who was in the killzone is a good defense."

"That has happened in some jurisdictions, but it won't here. I can persuade a jury to convict. Society cannot permit street justice."

I smiled in tacit disagreement. "Before the bit of street justice was carried out, did Meeks answer any questions?"

Adonal frowned. "What do you mean?"

"I mean before he was killed, was Meeks on a TC computer?"

The little color Ben had drained from his face. He blinked fiercely and grabbed the edge of his chair. "How did..." he said, then his tongue batted down the next syllable. "No comment."

"That's OK. I just wanted it confirmed and you just did." I sighed and pointed my finger at him. "The question is, why would any Liquidator ask questions of Wes Meeks? What would he possibly want to know? Is it true Meeks lied after the first question?"

A winter breeze from Ben's frosty stare blew through the room.

"Meeks was not a brave man. He would have lied only once," I said.

"Even if I knew what the interrogation was about, I couldn't tell you. The police and this office are investigating that conversation."

"Any chance of a mistake? That Wes Meeks wasn't the one killed."

Ben snorted. "Not a chance. It was Meeks. The bullet went into his heart, not his face. He was easily identified, but we did fingerprints and DNA too. Everything matched."

"But nothing is matching now."

I finished five miles on the blue, padded circular mat in the gym, then sat on a weight machine, preparing to lift. Sweat blotted my gray T-shirt. A towel hung around my neck. I used it to wipe the sweat beads from my chin. Being genetically modified is a plus, but you can't slack off. You still have to train, exercise, lift, kick, watch your diet, and stay off couches for long periods of time. A lot of geniuses have failed because they didn't work hard. A lot of genplus people expect their metabolism to carry them through life. It doesn't.

"Jerico. How about giving a girl a little assistance?"

I waved at Tiffany Rossler. She was stretched out on a bench, in a blue exercise suit, with her hands around an exercise bar. I was surprised there weren't a few guys around to volunteer to help her. Tiffany is a six-foot stunning blond with the bluest eyes this side of Valhalla. With genetics, we can program in beauty and brains although—surprisingly—some couples did not give their daughters high IQs. That wasn't the case with Tiffany, though. She's a bio-chemist who can also play Beethoven's piano sonatas with ease. I supposed she could have been a professional musician, but she loved science.

I spotted as she lifted the bar.

"Haven't seen you for a while, Jerico. How are you?"

"Get better every day," I told her, my hands gently under the bar.

While some couples short their daughters on intelligence, many value blond hair and blue eyes. Tiffany's brother was two inches taller than her, but had the same physical traits. If any city had a Nordic Gods contest, they would have won the trophy. Of course many other sons and daughters shared the same physical traits. At the turn of the century, perhaps some would have thought that chilling—a eugenic nightmare. Nothing so dramatic. Society just has a lot of blonds running around. It's no problem since most of them—at least the majority of those I've met—are as nice as Tiffany.

She groaned as she made the tenth lift.

"How many do you do?"

"I'm up to fifteen," she said.

"What dedication."

"What stupidity," she said. "But I told myself I'd tone up this year."

Ironically, many of those blond children resent the genetic typing and are often estranged from their parents. A few—disgusted with the endeavor—have permanently dyed their hair brown or black. An extreme minority have undergone eye transplants so they can look at you with a black or hazel gaze. Humans are odd. Always have been. I suppose they always will be.

When Tiffany headed for the pool, I stretched back on the bench and started to lift, grunting with each effort. After sixteen repetitions I slammed the bar back on its groove. Janice Waller, one of the assistants in the gym, walked by. She's a slim, dark-haired girl with a ready smile that promises to solve all of your problems, or at least those connected to the gym. She pulled up a stool. I grasped the bar again, but Janice leaned toward my ear.

"Thought I'd let you know that Teller Nance is roaming around."

"Oh, no. Is the ring open?"

"Yep. You know Jack's philosophy. If two guys want to mix it up, lift the ropes and see who wins. I thought I would warn you. Nance likes to challenge genrich men. He likes to see how he matches up."

I decided not to be pedantic and point out I was only genplus. "I can tell him the answer. He'll win a few and lose a few. It's that simple."

She smiled. "Well, sometimes testosterone doesn't yield to logic."

"They can cure that nowadays. If they toss you in prison, it's mandatory. It's easier to deal with prisoners with no sex drive, even though the guards are robots."

"Well, this is a gym and such things are voluntary. Nance isn't in the receiving line."

"If I see him, I'll politely refuse."

"Fine."

Sometimes genpoor folks want to prove themselves. Tell the world they're as good as the genrich crowd.

No, they're not. Not physically. Not in terms of IQ. When Nance was fifty, his reflexes would be halved, at best. The quickness and strength of a genrich individual might be down by 15 percent, or less. The latter's immune system would still be humming at maximum efficiency. If wounded or injured, he'd recover quicker. The eyes would not dim, the hearing would be just as sharp. The human race was creating a superior breed of human beings, for better or worse, and beating up an occasional genrich individual in a martial arts match wouldn't change that.

I planned to keep out of Nance's way. But he snuck up on

me and slapped me on the shoulder.

"Jerico, let's go a couple of rounds."

"No."

"C'mon, man. You like to train. You need to keep in shape. Gotta stay prepared." He balled up his fists and danced around, punching the air. He's about four inches shorter than I am, with curly black hair and dim green eyes. He also has the assertiveness of King Kong.

"Find someone else," I said.

His fists stung my shoulder. "Let's go. You afraid? Think I might beat you?"

I nodded. "That's probably it."

A left jab stung my shoulder again. I made a fist, but my reply was interrupted.

"Hey, poor boy. I'll take you on." Willy Hummerstun showed a cocky grin. His punch popped on Nance's chest.

Nance's eyes flared. He know what the "poor boy" reference was to. Will was genrich.

"Let's go," Nance said. He started walking toward the boxing ring.

Willy winked at me. "Thought I'd do you a favor, Jerico. Knew you didn't want to fight him, but I'd like to kick his butt."

"Give him an extra kick for me."

"Done."

I watch him walk away, stepping with the confidence of a genrich man who's also well trained. I wandered toward the ring. Nance reminded me of the bully in junior high, but at least Nance had one redeeming feature. He didn't pick on the weak and wanted a fair fight. He was annoying and obnoxious, but not totally devoid of character.

As I watched the two warm up behind the red ropes of the ring, I realized Nance had another problem. Being medium-height, he had a short reach. The two moved to the center of the ring. Nance started dancing, feigning punches. Willy balled his fists, sizing up his opponent. For a punch to connect, Nance had to move in. When he did, Willy's fist smacked him. Nance danced away, then moved back in, but his punch bounced off Willy's shoulder. Willy's left spun his opponent's head around. Two quick belly punches. When Nance twirled away this time, his knee slapped the mat. He was up quickly but took the rough end of the fury of punches that followed.

I had seen enough. I walked away. I figured the thud behind me was Nance hitting the canvas.

Fifteen

Before the doorbell rang, Francine told me there was an armed lady walking toward the house.

"But is she good-looking?" I asked.

Francine politely inquired whether the more important question wasn't one of firepower. Not when you have a computer that is also armed, I told her. I flicked the screen on and Sierra popped into view. Her smile radiated confidence. Of course, when you know how to handle guns and have an IQ a few points shy of 180, you have a great deal to be confident about. I studied her for a moment. How old was she? My age? A few years younger? I had never asked. Chronological age meant so little nowadays. I increased the power of the camera and studied her. No lines or wrinkles. A half-century ago, small lines would have appeared around the eyes and mouth. But it would be a long time before fleshly lines chipped away at her beauty. The lustrous red hair added to the Florida scenic landscape. The green eyes were deep and rich. Her small mouth could quickly widen into a huge smile. The smile could create a rolling cascade of infectious laughter. I wasn't sure if the flawless tan came natural or via genetics or by way of machines. I leaned toward natural. Even our high-tech tanning machines could not produce consistent all-over color. Her rich and supple figure was graceful both on the dance floor and on the firing range. Her brilliance, of course, sparkled even more fiercely than her green eyes. The only flaw she had was that off-center golf swing.

Lori had mentioned intercessory prayer in one of our talks. I didn't think much about it then, but now I realized how valuable that would be, if it works. I desired the best for Sierra. I didn't want to see her harmed in any way. Most friends can only hope for the best. If intercessory prayer is effective, we could help our friends even though we might be thousands of miles away. Steer them away from accidents. Or from bad relationships. Or make sure the bullet, instead of striking the heart, misses by inches.

I opened the door and greeted her. She showed her wide smile.

"Come to schedule another golf game?" I said, as we walked into the living room.

"I want to schedule something else."

She sat down on the soft. I eased down in a chair. I figured this was something she didn't want to say over cell phones or computers.

"I'm free for a weekend in the Bahamas," I told her.

"No, you're not. You're on a case."

"I can let that go for—"

"So am I."

I nodded. "And your case involves me?"

"Let's say our cases might converge. I think I might, in a few days, head out to the St. John's Clinic. The administrators have promised to give me an official tour—professional courtesy and all that. But I want to do a little unoffical business there too. Would you care to join me?"

I grinned. "I might like to see what's out there."

My response prompted another wide smile and a delightful wink from a green eye. "I will let you know when I'm ready. If you had said no, I would have had to make other plans." She looked around. "Not going to offer me a drink?"

I looked at my watch. "Actually, I have a client coming over."

"Ahhh," she said, giving a sensuous tone to the syllables. She stood up and patted my cheek as she walked by. "Another week in the Bahamas?"

"Walking on the beach," I said.

I escorted her to the door.

"We can schedule golf another time," she said.

"Keep your head up, when you're not swinging a golf club," I said.

"That's always good advice."

"Doesn't the heart know?" Lori asked, as we headed toward a small crest in the sand.

"Know what?"

A wind whistled along the shore and the waves slapped the sand with liquid fury. Water flowed to within a foot of us, then slid back on the darker, wet sand and receded into the sea.

"If you have a holographic female. I know some people become addicted to such fantasies, but that's not my area of expertise, but doesn't the heart know?"

She was dressed in a bright orange suit. Granules of sand spotted her body, with several grains near the small mouth. She wiped a wind-blown strand of hair away from her eyes. Flecks of the sea dampened us as we walked.

"You're a Christian. You should realize that the flesh is rather stupid. It doesn't want to know."

"Yes, that's true," she said. "Christians are aware we are a spirit, we live in a body and have a soul, which are the emotions, the intellect. As Christians, our spirits are reborn. We are one with Jesus. But even someone with what the Scriptures refer to as a dead spirit must realize the ... artificialness of it."

I shrugged. "When the flesh gets used to something, it's

hard to argue with. Plus, the holoaddicts tell themselves it's real. They don't want to know the truth." I looked at Lori and smiled. "They're very content with their dead spirit and stupid flesh."

"Until the fantasy breaks down."

"Yes, when they can't pay the utility bill, they are brought back to reality rather quickly."

"And some don't make it?"

"Some are unable to make the readustment to reality." I gestured toward the waves. "They walk into the ocean, or shoot themselves and, some, when they know the fantasy will fade soon, simply walk into a hologram, plug in, and die. It's rumored they die smiling. In a rather emaciated condition, though."

"Is real life so threatening and so frightening?"

"To some, it is. I guess."

"They need the Lord, they need Jesus. You don't see many Christians killing themselves like that."

"Not many. But once you start living a lie, it's difficult to come back to the truth. If a lie is easy on your mind and flesh, it's accepted. Humans, I suppose, can rationalize almost anything. By the way, is that a sin? Sex with an imaginary woman, or man? The Scriptures are—"

"Yes," Lori said defiantly. "It's selfishness, and sin is selfishness."

"Well, you're not hurting anybody."

"You're hurting yourself..."

"Possibly."

"You're living a lie."

We stopped and turned around. Her fingertips pressed against my bare chest. The eyes were curious.

"Did you ever have a fantasy that fixated you?" she asked.

"Not really. There was one I did a few times, for reasons I thought were justified. It wasn't a sexual fantasy, though."

"Care to tell me what it was?"

"No."

She groaned. "Why are you like that?"

"I think it's a guy thing."

"Ha! In the twenty-first century, men were supposed to be open, communicative, and sensitive."

"The Europeans were open, communicative, and sensitive. They died out."

She poked me in the ribs.

My two huskies met us when we returned to the house. I petted them, and they scampered along with us. I smiled as Jackie ran toward the waves. Granules shot up as she dug her paws into the sand. She halted at the edge of the surf, then trotted back.

I looked at Lori. "I have a question for you. Not psychological, but theological."

"That's not where my degree is, but I'll see if I know the answer."

"Humans go to heaven, correct?"

"Some humans. If you know Jesus. If the dead spirit inside you has been reborn."

"If we go, do we get to take our animals? Do dogs go to heaven?"

"I'm not sure theologians have pondered that question, but I can tell you what I think."

"Please do."

She smiled and tossed her head back. "I was driving one day while listening to a Christian radio station and this testimony came on. A woman mentioned her pet cat had died. She had had the cat for fifteen years and was depressed that her companion would no longer be with her. She was praying and she had a vision of heaven. There were all kinds of animals. Dogs, cats, horses. So she asked the Lord, 'Where do all these animals come from?' His reply was, 'These are the animals of the redeemed.' "

She smiled, then looked off into the horizon. Rembrandt would have enjoyed capturing her beauty on canvas.

"It's a wonderful story," she said. "Of course, we have to consider it skeptically because we don't have chapter and verse on the subject. But we do know there is at least one animal in heaven. Jesus will come back one day riding a horse. But if there's one animal in heaven, I think we can assume there are others."

"So you believe the story?"

"Yes, it resonates with my spirit. I knew that may sound strange to you...."

"No, it doesn't. Well, it does, a bit. But in my work I've found I need to trust experts from time to time, and you're an expert on God and Jesus. So I trust your judgment on the matter. That means there are animals in heaven."

She nodded. "I think so. It sounds like Jesus. It sounds like something my Father would do."

I had always thought of God as God, but Lori spoke of him with an intimacy that was beyond my comprehension.

I bent over and kissed her cheek. Her arms flew around my neck. I embraced her and the world disappeared. I never realized it had been so heavy.

I wondered if I should tell her about the spectre, the icy embodiment of death. Lori was warmth and life. I wondered if her fiery brilliance would melt the dark figure. I thought it might. But I stayed silent. It was enough to be in her arms.

Sixteen

Griff MacDowall was a solid-built, rock-slab of a man whose forearms made cement look weak. His dark hair was receding ever so slightly but, in back, the tangled curls went over his collar. I imagined he could be intimidating, but he never liked to scare people. He was gregarious and friendly to a fault. For a man who looked like a friendly bear, his voice was surprisingly soft, barely in the tenor range.

He only had one aggravating habit. At a table, if in thought, he would jangle his empty coffee cup on the saucer. He held two fingers around the holder, and flicked his hand back and forth. The discordant jangles weren't loud enough to be heard at the next table. However, I was sitting with Griff at his table, and the cup sounded like a hammer when it clanged against the saucer.

I couldn't blame Griff. I asked for a favor that, if discovered, could have him facing state and federal changes, in addition to bankrupting him.

His red-haired wife was as pleasant in personality as he was. The son was a sophomore at a local high school, and the daughter was in eighth grade and a budding ballet dancer. The fact that such a large and rough-looking man could have a ballet dancer for a daughter was of endless fascination to Griff.

It was wrong to ask him. He had too much to risk. But I knew if he accepted, the item would be delivered as swiftly and as efficiently as possible. He was my first choice, but I had told him there was no problem if he refused.

Griff owned the Sportsmen Gun Club and Shooting Range. His love for guns was only second to his affection for his family. He was also an expert on all types of weaponry, from about the fifteenth century on, although he specialized in small-caliber handguns and military rifles.

He edged back in his seat and stared out the large picture window. We were on the third floor of the Bay Inlet building, in the Golden Sands restaurant, facing the Atlantic. His hand kept flicking the coffee cup, making the discordant sounds louder. Fortunately, a waitress thought the clanging meant he wanted a refill. She rushed over and filled his cup with steaming black coffee. Griff sampled it, then winced. He picked up a spoon and flicked out a piece of ice from his water glass, dumped the cube in his coffee, then stirred it. The spoon rattling in the cup made much less noise than the previous jangling.

I drank some water and felt another stab of guilt.

Griff sampled the coffee again but this time smiled instead of wincing. "Since you asked this, I assume it's a matter of life and death."

"I think it very well could be."

"Why do you need those particular items?"

"I can tell you if it makes a difference."

"No," Griff said quickly. "I know you won't use them in any criminal activity. That means that, for some reason, you need them for self-defense."

I nodded.

"But armor-piercing bullets are very difficult to get. They're illegal, but I don't think that's the main problem. Not that many are being made, so they are very rare."

I nodded again.

"If found, they would be very expensive."

"Money, as they say, is no object. I would pay you a percentage."

"Not necessary."

"Yes, it is. Consider it a scholarship fund for the kids."

"Jim and Jodi have scholarship funds, but a little extra would never hurt."

"If you want to say no, go ahead. There are other sources..."

"Probably not as good or as trustworthy as I am."

"That's true."

The compliment made him smile. He was rock-solid in more than one way. "Since the bullets are so rare, they might be fitted to a unique caliber weapon, so you might have to buy a gun too."

"That's fine."

He drank his coffee and jangled his cup again. Another waitress approached, but he waved her off. He released the cup and sat back in his chair. "I'll tell you what I will do, Jerico. I'll make inquiries of certain individuals who will then make inquiries of certain other individuals. You understand I have never dealt in illegal commodities before, so this is unfamiliar territory for me. Because of my inexperience, this may take some time. If obtaining the items appears too risky, I will have to decline."

"I understand."

"If the items can be safely delivered, then I will do my best to secure them."

"Thank you, Griff."

Seventeen

"Yes, I remember Smokey. He was a good writer and an even better friend. I remember where I was when I heard about his death. It had that kind of an impact."

"You met him at college?"

"High school. Met him my junior year. We became fast friends. Even then he was focused on writing. Most of the class enjoyed film, videos, holograms, computers, but Smokey always loved the written word. I read many of his first attempts and read his first published story before it was sent to the *North Carolina Review*. It may have been an odd friendship because I enjoyed business and building things. I always liked to work with my hands. But Smokey and I both shared a love of adventure. He liked motorcycles, mountain climbing, scuba diving. He was a writer who didn't stay tied down to his desk. He was Hemingway without the bravado."

"Several news stories after his death quoted you and said you were his best friend."

He nodded. "I think that's right. He knew many other people and had a number of friends who were also writers and poets, but we always remained close."

"So you knew of his friendship with Munson Cain?"

"Yes. Cain came to speak at the university once. Surprisingly, he knew a professor who knew Smoky, and Cain asked to see him. He had read two of Smokey's stories and said he was impressed. It was an unlikely combination. Cain dreamed of the writer's life of action. Smokey lived it. But they both shared an appreciation of the written word. I always thought Cain behaved like a drunken frat boy, a rich drunken frat boy who knew there would be no consequences for his actions. But I will say this for him. He did appreciate good writers and helped them. He sent Smokey's stories to several prestigious journals, who published them."

"They ever get angry with each other?"

"They disagreed from time to time, but nothing serious. Even then we had heard of Cain's tirades but, with us, he was always pleasant and civil. I think he admired Smokey for more than just his writing. I don't think Cain was a brave man. Several times when we were diving, or riding or doing something with an element of hazard, Cain excused himself, always giving some plausible explanation. I think he admired Smokey's courage and audacity—*real* audacity, not New York literary stuff."

Edison Hathawat was the retired owner of a construction company. Francine had tracked him down after seeing his name in news stories about the death of Smokey Lansdale. He built and now lived in a large, coastal home on the ocean side of Currituck County, North Carolina. The Currituck Sound split the county into the mainland section and the beach section. Today, many of the construction jobs are done by robots, but Hathawat would fit right in with a construction crew. He would have worn a red S on his massive chest. The forearms bulged under the shirt. But the body slimmed down to an average waist. He puffed on a black pipe.

"On real cold winters, the Sound freezes over so you can walk to the mainland, if you want to walk over four miles of ice," he said.

I had wondered if, after so much time had passed, if anyone would recall Lansdale. Fortunately, he had been a unique character and Hathawat had a remarkable memory. He enjoyed talking about his friend. I hadn't seen his name among Cary's notes, but I guessed Cary would have found him eventually and interviewed him.

Hathawat continued, "Smokey, unlike many writers, was athletic. He handled motorcycles easily. He liked climbing mountains. Cain was the typical fumbler. He couldn't button his shirt without effort. Also, Smokey didn't really care what most critics said. There were one or two he respected, the rest he ignored. I think Cain treasured his press clippings. He lapped up praise but became infuriated when a critic panned his books. Smokey would take physical risks without fear, and literary risks too. I know there was only one element in his professional life that truly worried him. It was the only time I've seen him concerned."

"What was he worried about?"

Hathawat scratched at the corner of his mouth. "The one real fear Smokey had was being a one-hit wonder. He told me of musicians or writers who had one hit, maybe two, and then disappeared. I told him he had published more than two short stories, but he said short stories were okay, but novels were what really counted. He was really impressed with...I think it was Saul Bellow. A publisher had bought his first novel, but Bellow threw it away, thought it wasn't good enough. I think Hemingway might have dumped his first novel too. Smokey kept saying a writer should have more than one, or two, good novels to his credit. No one should be a flash in the pan. There should be a solid body of work for a good writer. In fact, he loved a story about John D. MacDonald. Know anything about MacDonald? He was a mystery writer back in the twentieth century."

I nodded. "Yes, I've read some of his novels. One of his main characters lived in Florida. His books reveal a great deal about the state at that time."

"Yes. Travis McGee. That was the name of his detective. I

think it was a publisher that suggested he write a series character. But MacDonald was aware of the downsides of using the same voice over a series of novels. He agreed to try to write the series, but wouldn't let his company publish any of the novels until he had completed three. He was writing the fourth before he allowed the first novel to be printed. He wanted to make sure he could maintain the quality of the books. Smokey really admired that. He said that showed the integrity of a true writer."

"Was he writing any novels when he died?"

He shook his head. "Not that I know of. He didn't talk about works in progress. A lot of writers don't."

"How did the accident happen?"

"He was riding on a mountain trail, as he often did. But it was just after a summer rain. He'd been riding for about two hours when he hit a slick spot. The bike skidded off and hit a tree. Death was instantaneous."

"I understand Cain gave a eulogy at the funeral service."

Hathawat flicked a lighter and relit the bowl of his pipe. Pine-scented smoke filled the room.

"He did, and I will say this for him, his memoriam was magnificent. Cain could use the language and his talk was an ode to a friend and colleague and fellow writer. He came close to comparing Southern boy Smokey to a minor god. It was not just an accident, but a Greek tragedy that such a promising life was cut short. The world was bereft and in sorrow. He compared the dew on the grass with tears of the earth, weeping for her young. Yet it was never corny, or pretentious. Cain spoke with sincere emotion. Anyone who heard him was geniunely touched."

I regreted the speech hadn't been filmed. It would be interesting to listen to Cain to see if I could be touched by his flowery words, especially since I knew how he managed to murder Cary Hallendorf. Not as difficult as I had first imagined.

Hathawat puffed on his pipe. "You know, I still miss him. We not only lost a good man, the world of literature lost a great writer."

And the world was left with Munson Cain. It wasn't a good trade.

Munson Cain was spouting more of his typical nonsense, then complaining in the next breath that no one listened to him anymore. Professors often listed his books on their must-read list but no university bothered to ask him to lecture anymore. I didn't bother to tell him there were good reasons why no one listened to him. The only question was why anyone ever did. In a world of cameras, there was no spotlight on him.

"They're afraid—everyone has been intimidated by this sterile establishment. Everything is computerized, robotized. It's not easy being a dissident in today's world."

"You've made millions of dollars and have three houses being a dissident. You're not a latter-day Solzhenitsyn. He risked his life repeatedly and spent eight years in jail."

"The obstacles are different in the United States but—"

"You're no longer on the lecture circuit because listeners got tired of your philosophy of selfishness and self-indulgence. There's nothing new in that message, but society always has younger, fresher voices to spread it. No wonder you like the 1960s. You'd been stuck there for decades."

Wind whipped through the curly hair. Nostrils flared. He clenched his fist and raised it. "I spoke of being authenically human, of—"

"You advocate acting like a three-year-old spoiled infant. Instead of self-indulgence, have you ever tried sacrifice? Helping people instead of strangling them? Have you ever done anything for anyone else without thinking first of Munson Cain, or, better yet, without thinking of Munson Cain at all? But I know the answer to that."

His lips parted into a feral snarl. He growled. "So what do you want here, Drake?"

"Thought I'd be here if you wanted to confess."

He eased back in his chair. We were at his Black Mountain home, on the outside balcony. The medical servitor stood behind him.

"There's nothing to tell."

"Yes, there is," I told him. "You killed Cary Hallendorf. First I wondered how. How an old, infirmed man could toss a young, strong one over a cliff. But I know how you did it. But I don't know why. What did Hallendorf find out?"

The eyes boiled. The color darkened, swirled, and shot black flares at me.

"They say the eyes are the windows of the soul. Want to know what your soul looks like, Cain?"

"Screw you. Cary liked me and he liked my work."

"He despised you, and everything you stand for. I know two righteous people, Cain. You ain't one of them. One works for justice and teaches Sunday School. The other is Cary's sister. Both are them are authentically human. Or maybe they're more than human. Perhaps both have a touch of the divine in them, something noticeably absent in you."

"You're nuts, Drake. I didn't kill Cary." A cruel smile parted his lips. "Even if I did, you can't prove it."

"There are rumors I'm a Liquidator. I wouldn't need to prove it."

Cain pushed back from the table and straightened in his chair. A slight tinge of yellow fear flashed across his face. He looked back, "Melvin would—"

"Do nothing," I said quickly. "He's not a Guardian. He's not programmed to protect you. Even if he was, he wouldn't be of any help. Guardians are like humans in one sense. Bullets can stop them. Shoot off a hand, and they will keep coming. Put a bullet in a leg and they can crawl. But put one or two bullets in the chest and the whole system is destroyed. Even if Melvin was a Guardian, I could pull my gun and shoot before he could make it over here."

I whipped out my gun and shoved the barrel under Cain's chin. A brief yelp of fear was gagged when the nozzle embedded in his throat.

"In your view, I am authentically human. After all, a robot wouldn't do this."

He opened his mouth, but no sound came out. Just fearful panting and a flickering tongue. Some animals can smell fear. It's a sweaty, musky scent, chilling and terrifying. It excites some predators, they feel that exhilaration of power, of control over others. Sometimes a scent of fear is mingled with their own sexual excitement. I only felt disgust. But criminals should feel some of the fear they have caused.

"My finger is on the trigger, Cain. Just one, gentle tug..."

Swear poured from him now. His hands shook uncontrollably. Tremors swept through his body. Then I slipped the gun back into my holster.

"If I ever become an evil overlord, I'm not going to give my enemy one last wish, or ask him one last question. I'm just going to shoot him. It's quicker and easier that way. But you, Cain, I want to live for a while. I want to know what Cary found out about you. I going to find that secret, then take you to trial and let you face the jury and all your friends."

I was halfway to my car when he regained his voice and started cursing me.

I looked back. Cain had fallen to the ground. His servitor helped him up and was walking him toward the house.

Delivering private justice is not a noble trait. I've wondered, from time to time, if I let it get out of hand. Adonal would not do it. Lori would be appalled. Giving in to bad habits can make them stronger. Would I become a bully of innocent people? I didn't think so. There had been lots of opportunities not taken. Even with Nance, I didn't take the bait. But every human lies to himself and deceives himself. In most cases, the lies are harmless. Was I fooling myself? Was I merely a slightly tarnished knight, or had all the white been worn off?

But when a criminal predator walks free, who mourns for the victims? Even more importantly, who will act for the victims? "Your brother's blood cries out to me from the ground," God told the original Cain. I heard a minister once who said such Scriptures are not metaphors. In the world of the spirit, blood has a voice. The blood of victims cry for vengeance. The blood of Jesus offers forgiveness, he said.

Christians such as Ben and Lori are in the forgiving business. That's not my profession. Evil seeks to extinguish the good. Sometimes in their confrontation with evil, the righteous need the service of the gray ones...like me. The gray ones are not pure light, but they keep the blackness from spreading. If they shed blood, it's not innocent blood.

Eighteen

Lori and I dove in opposing ends of the pool and smiled as we swam past one another in the blue waters. When I came to the end of the lap, I dove, kicked on the pool wall, and started back. Lori was already swimming my way. We patted hands as we churned water near the middle of the pool.

I climbed out first. I don't mind exercising but never enjoyed swimming for the sake of swimming. I walked to a yellow chaise lounge and sat down leaving damp footprints between the chair and the pool. Lori cruised several more laps before climbing out. She whipped off the bathing cap and shook her hair, then pulled at the bottom of the orange bikini, which was modest as bikinis go.

She eased behind me, towel across her shoulder, and laid back in the chair.

"So, you were going to ask me about a dream?"

"Yes, I was wondering if you might have any insights about it."

"I will do my best, if you will take me out tonight so we can celebrate."

"What are we celebrating?"

"My official graduation from UF with a psychology major and entrance into graduate studies," she said.

I whistled. "That is something to pop champagne over. Where you would like to go. Dinner? Movie? Auto racing?"

"Ha! No, I like the ballet and the local company has a show tonight."

I looked back at her over my shoulder. "The ballet?"

"You don't like ballet?" She gave me a fake forlorn look, lips drooping, sad eyes.

"Ah...I've always thought it was the epitome of creativity, innovation, and an expression of true artistic endeavor," I said.

Lori laughed. In a second she had eased next to me and threw her arms over my shoulder. She kissed the back of my neck while giggling. "Boy, you are good. Marvelous comeback. Hardly a hint of sarcasm. You don't like it at all, do you?"

"If I go with you, I will love it."

"He returns the shot with a great volley."

She scooted back on the lounge and extended her legs. "So tell me your dream and I will go into my psychology mode. I am a semi-expert on dreams. Is this one you had recently?"

"Yes. But the first time I had it was in my childhood. I've always remembered it, but had it again about a week ago."

"Tell me the details."

I sighed. "The central character is my grandmother, on my father's side, but it's strange because I don't remember ever seeing her. Her name was Amelia, and she died when I was two. In my neighborhood there was a house that, when I was young, always reminded me of a old Western log cabin. It had Western markings and a few decorations in Western decor. In the dream, my grandmother is in an old-fashioned buckboard in front of that house. She's in the back, with her legs tucked under her, and the buckboard is leaving. I know she doesn't want to leave, but she has to. There are two men driving. One, I think, is the leader. I see his face, and I know he's a hard man, not necessarily cruel, or even mean, but hard to be around, hard to work for. The other men is kinder. I hope he will take care of my grandmother. She is waving good-bye to me. I know I will never see her again. The dream ends there, with her waving me good-bye as she's being driven off. When I awoke, I felt an incredible sadness and loneliness."

"But you never knew your grandmother?"

"No."

"Were you told about her by anyone?"

"She was mentioned occasionally by the family. Amelia was a very loving, kind lady. Was a bit at odds with my mother, which is understandable considering the personality differences. Although mother preferred her eldest son, Amelia doted on me. I was told she was enamored of her youngest grandson…simply adored me. I wish I had known her."

"When did you first have this dream?"

"Shortly before Christmas when I was twelve."

"So tell me about your childhood around that time."

I groaned. "Do I have to?"

"If you want the dream interpreted correctly."

"I'm not sure it's worth it."

"Honey."

The snap of her fingers caused me to look back. She eased her legs to each side of the lounge. Her fingers motioned to me. "Lean back."

I edged back toward her, then leaned back. My head rested just below her chin. She brought her arms around me. Her wet hands patted my chest.

"Now tell me about Christmas when you were twelve. How can you be so specific about the date of the dream?"

"Because that Christmas is stark in my memory. It was the Christmas the family forgot about me."

"They forgot about you?"

I nodded. "Yep. Didn't get any presents. Everyone else did. I didn't. We had a Christmas tree and, like every child, I was curious. I checked the presents, looked at the tags, and a few days before Christmas, I told my mother, 'Mom, there's no presents for me.' She brushed me aside, saying, 'Of course, there are.' I said, 'No Mom, there really isn't.' She rushed by. She was always going someplace. On Christmas Eve night, when we opened gifts, there weren't any for me. My brothers and sisters were opening theirs, so I just eased out of the room."

"What did you do?"

"I went to my room and cried and cried. From the depth of my soul I wept. It wasn't just for the lack of gifts. I didn't care about the gifts, not really. The basketball incident I told you about had occurred about, oh, a month, six weeks before. At that time I felt, at least for a while, I was part of the family. I thought if it happened once, it could happen again. Things could change, and I could be more than a stranger in the house. That hope died that night. I knew I would always be alone."

I paused. Usually I don't like to talk about my past but being in Lori's embrace made it easier. "You know it's strange what the mind will do to you, the things you will tell yourself. Later that night, or, I guess, early morning, I told myself maybe I was hasty. Maybe there was something, even a small gift for me. Even a small present would mean acceptance. It would mean I was worthwhile. So I ventured out and walked down the stairs and looked beneath the tree. There was just wrapping paper and empty boxes. I sat down and starting crying again. I've never felt so lonely in my life as I did that night. But Scotty, our golden Lab, came out. Mother didn't like him in the house but, somehow, that night he was there. I grabbed him and hugged him, the tears running into his fur. He must have sensed something was wrong because he turned and licked my face. And it was better. It was not all right, but it was better."

Her lips kissed my neck again. "Jerico, I'm so sorry."

"I'm not complaining. I didn't lack for anything."

"Except love," she said.

"Yes, except that. But many, many kids grow up without love and poor, without love and without being genplus. Or were in an abusive household. All in all, life gave me a pretty good hand. There no use wasting time thinking about the past. After all, it happened when I was a child. Why worry about it?"

Her hands tapped my chest again. "Because sometimes events in childhood can influence our adult lives. Jerico, you are aware that your profession allows you to do in adult life what you did on that junior high school grounds long ago—protect the innocent from bullies. An action that produced the only compliment and affirmation of love from your father in your entire childhood."

"I'm aware of that. I'm not genpoor," I said, a little too sharply.

"I'm not saying you are. But even very intelligent people can be emotionally blinded when it comes to their own lives. You do see the correlation?"

"Yes, but it is coincidental. I lived on that compliment for months, years perhaps. But if my father would have praised me for beating up a smaller kid, I wouldn't have done it. We went to church, for show of course, but the minister often spoke of morals. No doubt I incorporated many of my values there, and from my own reading. Anyway, what does this have to do with the dream?"

"In the dream, how did you feel toward your grandmother when she waved you good-bye?"

"I loved her. I didn't want to see her leave, but I knew she had too."

"You didn't hate her for leaving you?"

"No, it wasn't her choice. Sometimes life is tough."

"The man in the dream you said was hard. Was he bigger and stronger than the other man?"

I thought for a moment. "Yes."

"And he was the leader?"

"Yes. I sensed he was."

"The other man, although kinder, was smaller and weaker?"

I nodded.

"So you're not angry at your grandmother for leaving, or at the human race or at God for taking away the only person who loved you, because life is difficult. But to deal with life you have to become hard, not mean or cruel, but hard and tough. The weaker man was gentle, a wonderful trait and perhaps he helped your grandmother on her journey, but he couldn't prevent her going away. So to deal with life you must became tough or you can't help others." She sighed and squeezed me with her arms. Her face lay against my back. "But you liked the weaker, kinder man better."

I moved my hands up and down her arms, then kissed her hand.

"I guess that's about the size of it," I said.

She kissed the back of my neck again. "Jerico, you mentioned once that you almost got lost in holographic space. But it wasn't sexual fantasies that you called up. Was it that time in your childhood, when you were happy playing basketball with your brothers and sisters?"

Her arms were around my neck. I kissed a slender wrist.

"Yes, I recalled and relived that time. For a while. But it wasn't the same, of course. You can't become young again. But Bill, Errol, Molly, and I laughed and played together...and there were no interruptions this time. I didn't really get lost in the fantasy, but I did call it up several times. Well, more than several times. But you can't undo the past. It was rather pathetic."

"No, it wasn't," Lori said. "You recreated a very happy time. It wasn't a sexual or violent fantasy, or a sadistic one, or a power or vanity fantasy. Adults remember the pleasant times and sometimes try to recapture them. If you're mature, you realize you have to move on. So it's not pathetic…just very human."

"I'm not human, I'm genplus."

"We are genetically advanced, Jerico, but we are still very human. Maybe more so than our non-genrich brethren."

"Now there's a horrific thought."

She laughed. "I was wondering....when I was at your house

and we were walking around outside, our of the corner of my eye I thought I saw a small monument with a figure of a dog on it. I was going to ask about it but got distracted."

I nodded.

"Is that Scotty?"

I nodded again. "Yes. He was about two that Christmas. Much later, when I got out of the army, I often visited him. He was getting older and didn't get much affection. I couldn't keep him at first because I just had an apartment.

"When I got the house, I took Scotty. Gave him the best food and the best care. He was about fifteen, sixteen at that time and getting arthritis. When I came home, we'd go walk on the beach, then he would sit down with me. Often he would wander down to the edge of the waves and stretch out on the wet sand. I thought the dampness would increase the aches, but Scotty seemed to enjoy it. After a few minutes, he'd stand up, shake himself, and be ready to run.

"Then one day, he was sitting on the sand next to me. He stood up, licked my face, then walked down to the tiny swirls and lay down. A few minutes later I noticed the waves flowing around him. I called to him, but he didn't move. I went down and touched him, but he was gone.

"You know, until then I thought it was silly to put a pet in a casket, but I didn't want to just throw dirt on him. I got a casket and buried him in the backyard."

"You like dogs more than humans, don't you?"

"Sometimes…often."

He was wonderful retriever with a golden, shining coat, an affectionate bark, and bright eyes. He liked humans even when they were none too kind to him. I stood before his grave and wanted to say something, a prayer I guess. But I didn't know any prayers and didn't know if God would listen if, in fact, there was a God.

"Good-bye, my friend," I told him. "I hope your last years

were happy."

"I'm sure they were," Lori said.

I didn't tell her of the second reason I called up the fantasy, because my rationale was silly and superstitious. But I've always thought if we had played a little longer, my life would have changed drastically. I thought the hot sun warmth of our basketball game would melt the icy, dark spectre. He could not have survived that afternoon, and his warning would have been empty. The wind would have blown his words away. If Mother had waited a few more minutes.... But if she had known about the spectre, she might have come out sooner, ensuring his victory. The warmth faded and the light waned. The spectre survived, and his icy warning was real.

When we went inside, I asked Lori to sit down. I mixed her a fake sloe gin fizz and sat it down on the coffee table before her. I told her there wasn't any doubt that Cary was murdered. Munson Cain killed him when Cary found out something the author wanted kept hidden.

She took a tiny sip of the gin. "Do you know what that was?" "Not yet, but I'm close to finding out. I have a few more trips to make. I think the secret is connected with Smokey Lansdale, and their alleged friendship. In fact, I'm wondering if Cary was the first person Cain killed."

That shocked her. She choked and gasped as if the pink gin had suddenly become vile. She tapped her hand on her chest and coughed.

"You think Cain killed Lansdale?"

"I wouldn't put it past him. He glorified violence and criminal behavior. Perhaps he had a fight with Lansdale. Officially, Lansdale died in a motorcyle accident. He was an active man who liked to ride cycles, but I still plan to look over the police reports."

"They would still have them from so long ago?"

"Yes, somewhere on a police computer, with written records stored away."

She was quiet. A curly strand of brown hair curled around her violet stare. She had more wisdom than most, but it did not come from her engineered genes. It was an odd moment for a epiphany but suddenly I believed in what she believed—there was something more to life than the physical. There was a God and, perhaps, even a Redeemer, although I still wasn't sure the race was worth redeeming. But if we produced a Lori, perhaps we are. Although humans and science didn't produce her. Her Lord did.

After minutes of silence, she said. "I want no vengeance. If there was a murder and you have evidence, you go to the police. The trail of blood must stop here. It's tough to forgive, but it's the only way. It's Jesus' way and His way is the only way."

Not on my side of town, honey, I thought.

"Also, I always thought no man was beyond redemption."

"You haven't met Munson Cain," I told her.

She gave a bitter smile. "I don't particularly want to." She shook her head. "I don't think I'd want to see him. I'm not sure my forgiveness would go that far but..." She raised her gaze and stared into my eyes. "I do not desire a Liquidator. I hired a detective and that's who I want."

I took a long swig of my drink. "Yes, ma'am."

Nineteen

Detective Henderson flipped open a file and stared at the white pages in the folder. She tapped the eraser end of a pencil on the pile. "So you believe you know how Cain managed it?"

I nodded.

She dropped the pencil in the file and leaned back in her chair. "What's your theory?"

"Hallendorf found out something about Cain's background, something that even Cain couldn't brag about or write about. He confronted Cain with it at the Black Mountain home. They were out near the ledge. I'm guessing there was a time when Hallendorf stood facing the valley, back toward the home. When you saw Cain he had a walker. He also had electronic wheelchairs and medical servitors. My guess is that day he was using two canes. Two sturdy, solid canes. He told Hallendorf he was recuperating from his hip replacements and there was no reason to doubt him. But surgeons are efficient today. I'm guessing Cain recuperated quickly from the operation. He didn't need the canes. But he walked slowly, as if he was weak and in pain. When Hallendorf turned away from him and looked out toward the valley, Cain grabbed one cane and swung it with all his might. He's about 180, 190 pounds over a squat frame. Even at his age, a roundhouse swing would knock you off balance. All Cain needed to do was knock Hallendorf forward. They were on the edge of the precipice. Probably Cain walked out there, luring Hallendorf to his death. He waited until his biographer was in the right position, then slammed the cane across the back of his head. It would be enough to knock him into the gorge and kill him."

"Yes. It's possible. Opportunity, but no motive as yet."

"I'm working on that. My computer tracked down the sister of Smokey Lansdale. She's in her eighties now, but very alert. She's the next person I'm going to talk to."

"If you find out anything, you will let me know?"

"If I can be there when you snap the cuffs on Cain."

"Deal."

"Will you rough him up a little?"

"We don't do that, Mr. Drake."

"Shucks. Makes you yearn for the good old days."

Griff had left a message for me when I returned to my house. After I walked Jack and Jackie, I phoned him back and told him to come over. Two hours later, his car pulled up on my driveway. When he got out, he carried a package.

"Francine, he will be carrying a gun, but you don't need to stun him."

"If he shoots you?"

"Then you can stun him, but I don't think you'll have to."

When Francine opened the door for him, I gestured for him to join me in my study, which is where I keep my guns. I eased into a chair as Griff opened the bag and placed the contents on the black walnut desk.

"There's not many armor-piercing bullets around, Jerico," he said. "But I got lucky."

"Glad to hear it."

"Out in the Western states there are a large number of gun enthusiasts and their enthusiasm extends to old West weapons.

They have clubs, stores, and shooting contests periodically to show off their skills. A few got curious some years ago about how powerful these weapons would be. Would an old colt be able to bring down a high-tech opponent? Sounds silly, but those are the questions some gun owners ponder. Akin to Medieval theologians pondering how many angels can dance on the head of a pin."

"Was that ever resolved?" I asked.

"Don't think so," Griff answered.

"Some time ago, a private firm created armor-piercing bullets used in some shooting contests. The contestants shot discarded robots. They wondered how many bullets it would take to bring them down." He shrugged. "Better than shooting harmless animals."

"Was that legal?"

"No crime to shoot a tin can." He reached on the desk and brought up an ancient weapon.

"A Colt .45," I said. "From circa 1877."

He nodded. "Fortunately not made in 1877. It's relatively recent, thanks to our friends out West who like new weapons. And these..." He opened a small rectangle box full of cartridges. "And armor-piercing bullets for it. Three dozen rounds."

"If that doesn't stop it..."

"Nothing will," he said.

Then he reached down and brought up the shining brown leather. I stood up and took the holster from his hands, then wrapped it around my waist. I slipped several bullets into the chamber of the .45 and eased it into the holster. Griff smiled.

"You look like a sheriff."

I grinned. "But I'm looking for something that didn't show up in the Old West."

"Something robotic?"

I nodded.

"I tested it for you, Jerico, with regular bullets. I didn't want to waste the others. It's a good gun. Shoots down the center, not to the right or to the left. If you aim well, you will hit the bull's-eye."

"I think mine will be a moving target. I don't think it will stand still."

"Good thing you're genplus. That adds quickness to the aim."

I nodded. I hoped it would be enough.

Of course, maybe Mullet was spinning a line. He saw some money down the line and was fabricating the whole story. Next week, he would say he could get Barlow to sabotage the alleged robot for, say, twenty-five thousand dollars. Give him the money and the robot and the threat disappears. Just a huge scam by Mullet, but a good one.

But I didn't think Mullet was lying. The Jackal was out there. It was the icy spectre materialized on the physical realm. It was the Grim Reaper with glowing red eyes. My appointment in Samarra was rapidly approaching.

Twenty

Rachel Lansdale Langley had a private room in the Sunnydale Mountain Facility, a long-term, rehabilitative medical complex. She was eighty-one and her left arm was partially useless due to a stroke. We sat on a small balcony that overlooked shuffleboard lanes, a bike path, and hilly lands. Alert eyes and a bright smile redeemed a plain face and listless hair. But she was happy to have a visitor who wasn't her family. Thankfully, the medical servitors are very inexpensive in regard to long-term maintenance. They cost less per year than the average human worker and provide excellent almost-human care. Before the servitors took over, the care of the elderly became very expensive to society. So, by the oddest coincidence, the elderly began dying quickly in long-term facilities and, in fact, in their family's homes. A hedonistic society has no use for those who are not part of the pleasure games.

"Smokey's death was a great loss, and not simply because he was a writer. My brother Dan, Smokey, and I loved one another and we came from a close-knit family. Since he died, there's always been something missing. You can't replace a brother or sister, or a loved one. I still have his picture there on the dresser."

"May I look at that?"

"Of course."

I realized I had never seen a picture of Smokey Lansdale. I walked over and looked at the dozen photographs mounted in small, golden frames. One showed a much younger Rachel, a much younger Munson Cain, and another young man. He towered three inches over Cain, had a muscular chest, and strong arms. A lighter blond than his sister, he shared a dazzling smile with her. Both had dark eyes but fair skin. I had assumed writers were introverts, spending their time with books and imaginary characters. But Smokey had a gregarious look. I could see him riding motorcycles, scuba diving, or jumping from airplanes.

I returned to the balcony and sat down. "He was a very good-looking man."

"Yes, he was. We kidded Smokey that he got the looks in the family, and the talent. He was always an active child. He enjoyed playing football and baseball, but he was also an avid reader. He devoured books, as I suppose most writers do, but he was never a loner. He was always surrounded by friends, played high school football and baseball. Some of the best friends he had up until his death were his former teammates."

"When did he meet Munson Cain?"

"Second year of college, although it wasn't officially his second year. I think Smokey would have been a success in whatever he tried, but he determined in junior high that he wanted to be a writer. After high school, he took two years off just to experience the world. And I do mean experience. He wandered through the nation, finding odd jobs, meeting people, seeing the sights. There were no grants, no government handouts. But he treasured those two years, always said he felt his writing would have been poorer with them. Then he entered college but really wasn't satisfied with the academic environment. The second year he was simply taking a few English and writing courses, excelling at them but felt uneasy with what he felt was the pretense and phoniness there."

"But he had already sold several stories, right?"

She nodded. "Two regional publications had purchased his

stories and his novella *Waves of Silence* had been sold but not yet published. The novella gained him some critical acclaim. But Mr. Cain read his first three short stories and was tremendously impressed. He was at the university to give a lecture and wanted to meet Smokey. They liked each other immediately, although Smokey liked everyone. Although he sometimes gave his characters nefarious motives, he seemed to believe the best of real people. An odd trait for a writer."

"Yes, it is."

"Mr. Cain asked him if he had any other short stories. He did and, after some talking, Cain convinced Smokey to let him send it up to the *Maine Quarterly*, which accepted it without reservation. I was with Smokey at our house when Cain was in another room reading *Waves.* When he finished he literally came running out, the typed pages in his hand, slapped the manuscript on the wall, and said, 'This is brilliant! It's some of the best prose I've ever read. Have a drink around here?' We poured him some Scotch. He downed it in one gulp. 'Incredible. Smokey, you're the best writer I know. Lemme have another,' he said, stetching his hand out with the glass. 'You're one fantastic writer. A lot of critics are praising writers who shouldn't be allowed to hold your pencils or shine your computer screen.'"

"Did the friendship continue?"

"Oh, yes. To the day of Smokey's death. At that time, Munson wasn't as...outrageous as he later became. He had some human traits. We grew up Baptists and occasionally Smokey would say of Munson, 'There's a great writer in there if he doesn't let the flesh get in the way.' But Munson did. He let the flesh—publicity, ego, and alcohol get in the way. He did get out three good novels, though, but I don't think he would have written those if he hadn't met Smokey. In Smokey's last story, you see a slight influence of Cain, but in Cain's Southern trilogy you could see a great deal of Smokey's influence."

"Your brother never attempted a novel?"

"Not that I know of. I knew he would have if he'd lived. You know, Smoky was something of a perfectionist. I think he wanted to make sure he had mastered the short story and novellas before starting a novel. I wish he had. We only have his six short stories and *Waves.* Would you like to see where he wrote, like the last fellow?"

I shifted in my seat. "The last fellow? Who was that?"

"A very nice young man named Cary Hallendorf. He was interested in Smokey, said he was writing a biography of Munson Cain."

I nodded.

"We grew up around Cove Creek, a small town southwest of Asheville, but the folks retired to Florida and Smokey took up residence there. In fact, no one has lived there since Smokey used it. Smokey liked people, except when he was writing. He wanted solitude them, so the isolated farm house was perfect for him. When he died, we rented the grounds out to tenant farmers. Every year they grow three crops of hay and sell it to surrounding farms for feed. Smokey liked the house, he said it was a good place to write. He did have one odd trait. He didn't write on a computer, but on an old word processor. It was old when we were growing up, but Smokey found it in the attic when he was about twelve and for some reason liked it. Cleaned it up, dusted off the disks, and slid them in the slot. He began typing stories, or at least notes, on that machine and never quit. He made a study out of a second-floor room at the house. He could look out the window onto the green hills. I know he liked to write first thing in the morning. Sometimes he watched the sun come up from that room. The house was deserted, so it fit his need for solitude when writing. He never let anyone come in with him, not even friends. He wanted peace when he wrote. He would often drive, or ride his motorcycle, fifty or a hundred miles to get to the house. That was nothing to Smokey."

"You told this to Cary?"

"Yes. He wanted to visit. We have a friend who keep tabs on the place now. Mike Sandforth. He's the son of a boy we grew up with. I phoned him and he let Cary in. Would you like to see the house too?"

"I think so."

She pointed to a cell phone on the table. "If you will dial for me, I'll tell Mike you're coming."

The Lansdale farm was twelve miles outside of Cove Creek, and down three miles on a dirt road. The house was surrounded by trees. Three large fields, guarded by oaks and weeping willows in a dozen varieties of green, surrounded the house. I opened the door and walked in. Boxes were piled everywhere. A sofa and several chairs, covered with dust, stood in the front room. Two steps in and the staircase began. I thought the architecture was odd, but the house must have been 150 years old. Maybe that's how they built them back then. A second room held a lounge chair, a desk and lamp, and bookcases. The kitchen held a stove and an off-blue refrigerator. I flicked on the lights and discovered there was still electricity.

I walked up the stairs. Only four small rooms were on the second floor. Two bedrooms, a third room, and Smokey Lansdale's study. His desk was by the window. I was surprised to see what I assumed was an ancient word processor on the desk. I opened the drawers. Empty except for several cartons of discs.

"That's odd," I said.

A layer of dust was in the room, but the word processor and the cartons were clean. Someone had wiped the dust off. I noticed the black cord from the processor was inserted into a wall socket. I pushed a square red button. The machine sputtered on. The screen flashed white, then changed to a dull gray before words formed. A plastic green wastebasket by the desk held crumpled paper. I reached in and took one out, unraveling it. Paragraphs and sentences.

There were two discs laying beside the machine. I took the first one and inserted it. The menu surprised me. I punched a folder and a page came up, with a familar title.

And I knew what Munson Cain had to kill to protect.

I flipped open my cell phone to call Detective Henderson. She would need to go through all the evidence, then get a warrant. But I wanted to see Cain first and tell him his secrets would soon be revealed.

In late October, the North Carolina landscape is bleak and dark. Cain stood on the ledge outside his Black Mountain home. On my first trip the leaves had been changing. The forest background was a mixture of reds, yellows, greens, and an odd shade of orange. The colors gave viewers a surge of hope. Beauty and serenity. Now the leaves had fallen and the trees offered bare, pointed branches to the sky. Hope had vanished like the leaves. The wind bristled through the bare branches, rolling off the mountain sides, screeching as if in agony as I walked out to meet Cain.

He didn't have his canes and looked stable on his feet. Dark pants, a shirt, and only a light jacket. Being macho to the end? I wore a thick, gray jacket with the collar turned up. Cain looked as ugly as the landscape. His lips formed a scowl. The dark eyes glared with hate as I moved toward him. I stopped when I was about three feet from him.

"Why are you here, Drake?"

"Oh, I just wanted to gloat. Not a Christian trait, but neither of us are Christians are we, Cain? Expecially you."

He looked away for a moment and spit into the dirt. "Gloat? About what?

"There was never much doubt about who killed Cary Hallendorf. The question was how and why. I explained to Detective Henderson how, but the why remained open. What secret did the very public Munson Cain want kept in darkness? What are even criminals ashamed of?"

"Screw off and die."

"Not yet, Cain." I stepped closer to him. "Cary, that diligent young biographer found your secret. Your friend Smokey Lansdale only had one fear. He climbed mountains and dived in the ocean, rode motorcycles, and who knows what else. But he did not want to be known as a one-book wonder. He wanted a solid literary reputation. He never told anyone, even his agent, that he had written two novels and was completing a third. When he typed the last chapter on the third novel, he would have told the world. Until that time, he only let one other man read his novels...his good friend Munson Cain."

"This is fantasy."

"No, tragedy. A writer—even a writer as limited as you—should know the difference. Munson Cain. Fraud. Charlatan. He took another man's works and built his reputation on them. I just have one question."

Cain turned away from me and stared at the mountains. "It's a lie."

"No, it's not. Your reputation is a lie, and it will soon come crashing down. Detective Henderson has the word processor where Cary wrote his novels. You, I'm guessing, had the manuscripts. The motorcycle accident—that's what I'm puzzled about. Was it really an accident, or did you kill him?"

Cain turned his gaze back to me. There was anger in his face, and bewilderment. He snorted. "You are an idiot." He took a deep breath. "I told Smokey not to ride that day. It had just rained and the roads were too slick. He was riding on country roads that didn't have the safety protections main highways have. But he didn't listen. He had just finished a very productive couple of days of writing, and he wanted to get out. Feel the wind on his face. So he climbed on his cycle and took off. I was ten miles away when he crashed."

"So it was after his death that you got the idea of putting your name on his work?"

"His novels were exceptional. A guy like Smokey comes along once in a generation. The novels were just sitting there. He brought them to my apartment one day. Said he had a surprise for me, and did he. He wanted my opinion on them. He told nobody except me. Then he was killed. No one knew about the novels. So there was no reason not to take them."

"Excepting morals or ethics."

"Even a robot can be programed to act morally," Cain said.

"Yes, a line from one of your later works. Therefore, men should be freed from moral restraints. Be his own god."

"Yes. At least I've lived my philosophy. I'm not a hypocrite."

"A murderer who kills again may not be a hypocrite, but he's still a murderer. There are things worse than hypocrisy."

All I got was a scowl from him.

"There's a robot back in Florida who may be a murderer but he can't be a hypocrite, You're as empty inside as he is. Your entire philosophy is based on not being a mechanical man but you're very much like one. No morals, no compassion, entirely selfish. No wonder you loved the "60s'. Where there should be a living spirit inside you, there's just a dark hole."

I looked out toward the bare valley. "I'm going to expose you, Cain. You stole another man's work. Maybe you had talent at one time, but Lansdale was a better writer. He was also a better human being, and that gave his writing some transcendence. He will be remembered after your books and essays will be forgotten. When this is revealed, your name will be laughed at and scorned."

When I looked back, Cain's hand was inside his jacket. I guessed what the bulge under his armpit meant.

"Don't be a fool," I told him.

His hand wrapped around the gun and pulled it from the holster. I took one step. My disgust turned into fury. He groaned as I kicked him squarely in his chest. He fell back and rolled to the end of the ledge, grabbed for a non-existent guardrail, and yelled as he went over.

I rushed to the edge and looked into the canyon. I guessed Cain had landed not far from where Cary Hallendorf had fell.

"You second-rate hack. You can't even die right," I said.

I shook my head. Lori loved her brother, but she would never forgive me.

Twenty-one

I was glad for the call from Sierra. I didn't want to face Lori yet. I'd rather face the Jackal than tell her what had happened in Black Mountain.

Sierra was stretched out on a huge blue blanket with a yellow beach umbrella overhead. I didn't see why she had the umbrella because she was in the sun and not moving. I guess the temperature was in the high 70s on a cloudless day. She wore a bright blue bikini, held together by small gold rings. Several men eyed her as they walked by, but her focus was on the book she was reading. She turned the pages quickly. Like most genrich folks, Sierra is a speed reader. I've seen her scan scientific manuals—an awesome sight—while picking up every scientific detail. When she looked up, I waved. She stood up, grabbed a huge yellow towel, and walked toward me.

She eased down opposite me, and took off her sunglasses, then wiped her face with the towel. We both ordered drinks.

"Thanks for coming," she said.

"At your beck and call."

A waitress brought her a large Margarita. Sierra sipped it. "We're ready to go into the St. John's clinic."

"I never did think you were down here just for a vacation."

She smiled. "Wow. You're good. I bet you got the platinum detective license instead of just the regular certificate. We go in today. This afternoon at two." Her eyes narrowed, and her voice dropped. "Once we get in, all bets are off. Be ready."

I nodded. "Will Cheruba be with us?"

She smiled again. "Not with us, but he will make his presence known. Let's say he may be at the back door, while we walk in the front. You can be my...security. We need protection with all those anti-genetic Luddites around."

"We will be checked."

"No problem for me. We'll have to change your computer files."

"The Blue Ridge Clinic can do that? I thought you were strictly scientific."

She dropped the straw in an ashtray and sipped the drink. "We're flexible. When St. John's checks your prints and your eyes, they will be a match for one of our security people."

"Then I need a new name too, to go along with the new resume. How about Cabot Alistair Lodge, IV?"

She frowned. "You don't look like a fourth-generation Lodge."

"What do you mean? How do they look?"

"Not like you. You can be Harry Jones."

"Jones? Jones?"

"It's a good name. Very common. That can be helpful."

"And Harry?"

"You look like a Harry."

"Shucks. I always wanted to be a Lodge."

"Only in holographic dreams, dear," she said. "Would anyone at the clinic know you on sight?"

"Doubtful. Daytona Beach is a big city and Volusia County has more than a million people. I've only met a few. If Meeks is there, he'd know me."

"But he won't be checking security at the door."

"I doubt it."

She raised her drink. "To you, Harry."

"They won't mind us carrying guns?"

She shook her head.

Twenty-two

"You killed him?"

I opened my hands, as if in surrender. "It was an accident, Lori. I swear it. I didn't mean to kill Cain."

Her eyes flared with anger. "Why did you go to meet him? Why didn't you just call the police and have them talk to him?"

"I...to finish the case. I needed to see the case to the end."

The words faded under her intense gaze. Violet lasers penetrated into my mind and soul.

"That's not why you went," she said.

I sighed. "OK, I wanted to confront Cain. I wanted to watch his eyes and see his reaction when I told him I knew that he had lied for fifty years about his three best novels...that his three best novels were not his."

"I didn't hire you to kill Cain, or kill anyone—"

"I didn't mean to, Lori. I...I.." I took a deep breath. "I didn't intend to kill him, please believe me. I did not go to that house to kick him off the ledge."

The air bristled with her indignation. "You're young, genplus, and a professional. You had to kill an old man!"

"An old man who murdered your brother," I yelled. "A godless, cruel killer, who was shrewd enough to bash Cary when his back was turned."

"You didn't have your back turned to him."

My heart pounded. I closed my eyes briefly. "No, I didn't. I told you once, Lori, that professionals can never get angry or they make mistakes. I got angry at Cain, angry that he was such a useless, good-for-nothing fool. When I saw him reaching for a gun, all my fury went into the kick." I opened my mouth to say more, but no words came out.

Lori turned around and looked out her patio window. She crossed her arms. "You're a very charming man, Jerico, and in some ways...but I was mistaken." She shook her head. "I think you should go."

"Lori, please believe--"

"*I think you should go now.*"

I nodded and walked toward the door. Her curt voice stopped me as her computer opened it.

"Jerico." She stood before the window but turned to face me. "I don't think you should come back."

Back home I petted the dogs. I sat on the sun porch on a wooden chair and stared into the ocean. Jack and Jackie knew something was wrong. They stretched out on each side of the chair. My hands were in my lap. I raised my right hand when I felt the moisture. The droplets formed a crude pattern across skin and bones. At first, I looked at them with a puzzled and baffled gaze. I hadn't seen such things for twenty years, not since that long ago Christmas when I hugged Scotty.

Another difference between humans and robots.

Robots don't cry. Perhaps I should have mentioned that to Cain when I was up in North Carolina. Cain was much closer to robots than he thought. They don't feel shame or guilt, and neither did he.

The cell phone buzzed me out of my oppression. I flicked it open, and Mullet popped up on the small screen. He said it was an emergency.

We met at a private booth at the Driftwood, but this time I bought him an early lunch. I sipped my drink as he chewed his way through the prime rib.

"Excellent food here, Jerry. One of the best restaurants in the state." He tapped the meat with his fork. "Never had anything this good."

"Is this about the Jackal?"

"It sure is. It's almost ready. A day or so, and they will let it go."

I didn't bother to tell him it didn't matter anymore.

He pointed his fork at me. "It's not just after you, although Meeks does hate you with a passion. He still thinks you killed his son. But he also wants your friend, the state attorney, and your other friend."

"Ben?"

"Yeah. He was leading the charge to prosecute Wes. Meeks wants him dead too."

"I supposed something evil would go after the righteous. But what do you mean about my other friend?"

"The girl. Meeks has had you watched. He knows you're seeing what's-her-name—Leigh, Lori..."

I grabbed a fistful of his shirt. "What?"

'Hey, it's not my fault. It's not me, Jerry. I'm just telling you what's happening."

"I'll kill Meeks."

"Or he'll kill you."

"You're not lying to me, are you, Mullet?"

He raised both hands, a knife in one hand and a fork in the other. "Why would I do that, Jerry? If they knew I'm telling you this, that thing comes after me."

I eased back in my chair. "How long?"

He nodded. "A day. Two days. Can't say for sure. The way I heard it they want to kill Lori first, to make you suffer, then kill you and Adonal."

"When? What are their plans?"

He shook his head. "Don't know specifics. From what I gather from Barlow, the Jackal is distinctive. That may be good, but it also means it can't be in public. It has to stay hidden during the day. Like a real jackal, it comes out at night."

"Weapons. How is it armed?"

"Doesn't need to be. It's strong. It's much stronger than any human, even genrich humans on steroids. They may have given it a holster and gun, just for emergencies. It could strangle a lion."

I drove to Lori's house, ran to the front door, and knocked frantically.

The computer responded. "She is not here, and you are no longer on Lori's entry list. Please remove yourself from the premises, or I will stun you."

"Robert, Lori is in danger. Where is she?"

"I am not programmed to tell you about her movements. Now please remove yourself from the premises."

You can't argue with a robot armed with stun lasers.

"OK, OK, I'm leaving. But your owner is in danger. Check your files. You know my name and my profession. So when I tell you that Lori is in danger, it should be credible."

The computer paused.

" When she returns, please have her stay here, inside. How's your security?"

"Top-flight."

"Your lasers?"

"Can slice through a tank."

"Good, they may have to. By tonight, she will be safe."

The computer paused again. "I will send a message to her. When she returns, I will be on high-security."

"Thank you, and will you tell her one more thing when she gets back."

"What message would you like to leave?"

This time I paused. "I know it doesn't matter to her, but tell her I'm sorry, and I love her. And...I hope she has a wonderful life."

Twenty-three

We walked into the St. John's Clinic a little after two. The monitors beeped and glowed red, but the regular security staffers were not alarmed. They had been told of our weapons. I didn't see the results of the fingerprints and retina scans, but the sullen watcher who viewed the screen didn't change expression so I assumed Harry Jones' profile showed up on screen.

After we exited the screening, we exchanged greetings with a vice-president, who introduced us to a medium-height, partially bald man in a white coat. He rushed up to Sierra and offered his hand.

"Dr. Cassi. Harold Theobault. You may not remember me but we met at..."

"The conference at Charleston earlier this year, on the consequences and benefits of cloning," Sierra said, affection flowing like waves in her voice. The vocal ripples washed over him and brought a huge smile. "I must say, Dr. Theobault, I thought your comments were right on the mark."

"Thank you. Please call me Harold."

Harold practically elbowed me out of the way as he edged closer to Sierra. She towered over him by at least two inches.

"I'm so glad you agreed with me that the cloning ban is silly," Harold said. "There's no reason to be uncomfortable with cloning." His mouth moved, but his eyes were fixed on Sierra.

I wondered if I should tell him that she didn't go for middle-aged bald guys.

She put her hand on his arm. "Could you guide us around?"

"Be happy to," he said, as he patted her hand.

She used her other hand to point to me. "This is Harry Jones, one of our clinic's security staffers. He's accompanying me due to all the threats we've had from the fundamentalists, both religious and secular."

"Vile people," Theobault said, still ignoring me. "I can understand, to a degree, the religious opposition, but the secular passion against genetic engineering has always baffled me."

He walked down the corridor while providing a running medical commentary. The facility was a three-story, high-tech environment that I guessed covered about six acres with the buildings and the grounds. Several Guardians passed by and I spied a security laser or two, but the facility didn't seem as well-guarded as a prison, or a high-walled suburb. Most of the heavy stun lasers were on the outside, protecting the scientists from vandals and the random antigenetic lunatic. Theobault droned on, his monotonous tone broken only by a occasional comment from Sierra.

After thirty minutes of touring, we passed a unit with two black Guardians securing the door and two red-tipped security lasers. Theobault pointed to the door.

"Some medical research must remain confidential," he said. "You'd be surprised how much spying and medical espionage there is today."

"No, I wouldn't," Sierra said.

Theobault excused himself for a moment to talk to another technician.

Sierra edged closer to me. "Anytime now," she said.

I nodded.

The explosion rattled the walls and the floor. It came from another part of the facility but echoed down the corridors. A piercing wail of a siren blared. Red lights flashed.

"Intruder!" a robotic voice yelled, before the next syllable died in a second blast. I grabbed the wall for support. Sierra wobbled on shaky legs, then found her balance. The Guardians stumbled, caught their footing, and started toward the sounds.

I grabbed my gun. "Cheruba does good work."

"Sure does," Sierra said.

She whipped her pistol out and fired at the retreating Guardians. One black head exploded after another. I fired at the lasers and watched them explode.

White-coated doctors, technicians, lab assistants, and a random employee ran toward the exits. Another fiery blast lifted up a Guardian and split the black figure into three parts, each spitting red and blue lights. A sprinkler system started spurting water that drenched my shirt and face.

Sierra reached into her jacket and brought out what looked like black clay. She smeared it on the door, stepped back a half dozen steps and fired. The clay exploded and the door shot out a thousand splinters.

We raced into the room. The corridor split into two pathways. Sierra sprinted to the left. A Guardian walked from an adjoining room and pointed his gun at her. I fired. Three bullets caught him in the back and propelled him into a wall. Sparks flickered from the wounds. Instead of blood, dancing orange light flowed from the dark figure. He turned toward me, then slumped to the floor.

Sierra was no longer in sight. The jarring, high-pitched siren wail reverberated in the building, then was muffled and became a series of intermittent moans. I ran down the hall, not sure what I was looking for.

But a second later I saw it.

And was stunned.

He lifted his weapon and fired. A thumping sound propelled the bullets. A flash of wind flowed over my ear as the slugs crashed into the wall behind me. My shot caught him in the chest. He spun around, smeared a wall with blood and was dead before he fell.

For a second I wondered if I was mistaken. I walked to the body and stared at it. I grabbed his face and yanked it right and left, as if it were a mask. Water dropped from my chin onto his face and his wide-open eyes. They didn't blink, and never would again.

A dead body with the face of Wes Meeks stared up from the floor.

But Wes Meeks was already dead.

OK, Drake, think. You're genplus. Use that abiilty.

Merrill Meeks owns a medical facility. His son has constantly been in trouble with the law and has a penchant for violence, particularly violence against women. Merrill can't buy off the local prosecutor, not when the local prosecutor is Ben Adonal. Even if he does there are Liquidators around, so Wes' violent hobbies could prove fatal. If so, there's no heir. End of the line. But Merrill thinks ahead. Years ago, he realized he might have to have a backup. Someone to die for his wayward son.

Or something to die for Wes.

A clone.

A clone so the real Wes could inherit and keep the line going. But if you create a clone it would take twenty-five years for it to grow and look like Wes. Another explosion and several gunshots grabbed my attention. Screams came from down the hall. I wiped the water from my face. I looked around, but the corridor was empty.

Somehow the facility had discovered the way to add growth compounds so they could build a clone in years, or even maybe months, instead of decades.

Pyogira.

What Sierra was investigating.

You couldn't tell which was the real Wes and which was the clone unless...unless you hook it up to a TC computer and ask some questions. Which is what Cheruba did and learned he had killed a clone. He must have suspected something or he would not have bothered with the TC. Or Sierra suspected something amiss and alerted Cheruba.

I whirled around at the first syllable of the anguished groan. The four men were not armed. The older one walked to the fallen man.

"Wes!"

Merrill Meeks slumped to his knees and put his hands on the chest of his son. Blood stained his fingers. He looked older than he did in pictures. Lines crisscrossed his face like battlefield trenches. His white hair had lost its luster. Pockets of gray stubble lined his cheeks. Tears flowed as he shut his eyes and gave another agonized sob.

Then Meeks looked up and fury replaced sorrow. He glared at me as he stood. "The Jackal will kill you for this. He'll make you pay."

I pointed my gun at him, but he simply shook his head.

"It doesn't matter if you shoot. I'm already dead."

"Not as dead as you're gonna be."

I lowered the gun and fired. The bullet glazed his thigh. Blood spurted from the wound. Meeks shrieked, grabbed his leg, and crumpled to the floor. I whirled and stuck the barrel at the temple of a white-coated attendant.

"That was to get your attention. Where's the Jackal?"

Sweat poured from the attendant's forehead.

"It's loose. We let it out."

"Where is it?"

"At the toxic waste site."

I thought a moment. "Daytona Atomic? That one?"

He nodded. "It was told to stay there during the day and come out at night. We knew no human would go in there. It was too dangerous to keep it here."

"And what," I said, grabbing his white jacket and pulling him closer to me, "are his orders?" I ground the barrel into his temple. He winced with pain. The barrel left a glowing circle of red on his skin.

"Meeks ordered us, he told us what to program the Jackal," he said quickly.

"What were the commands?"

"To kill a man named Jerico Drake, to kill his girlfriend, Lori Hallendorf and to murder Ben Adonal. He is the assistant—"

"I know who he is."

"We had to. Meeks—"

"You didn't have to," I yelled. "You chose to. There's a difference." I glared at the line of white coats. "If I don't get to the Jackal before he gets to Lori, you all have chosen to die." I looked at him, then stared at his colleagues, and waved the gun at them. "If she is hurt, I will come back and kill all of you. *Every last one of you.*" I wanted to shoot them all. "But because of Lori, all of you will stay alive...for now."

I gave him a savage pull and tossed him on the floor. I eased back down the corridor, through the sprays of water and the exploded bits of rumble now on the floor.

By the time I got to the exit, several police cars and two blue-and-white ambulances were on the scene. Sierra dabbed at a spot on her forehead. Blood flowed from the cut and onto her cheek.

"How's Cheruba?" I asked.

"Wounded," she said, glancing at the ambulance.

"Serious?"

"I don't think so."

She took a step but stumbled and gasped. Her hand went to her side. I grabbed her.

"You OK?"

"Got in the way of a Guardian."

I waved to the EMR technicians. They rolled a stretcher over and eased Sierra in it. Before they put her into the ambulance, she reached for my hand.

"Thanks," she said. "I saw what you did to that Guardian. You saved my life."

"Forget it. You would have done the same for me."

She squeezed my hand. "Maybe...Jerico, I knew, of course, what Cheruba was doing down here. I should have told you. Several times I almost did. I just ... just always failed at the last minute. It might have made things easier for you.

I kissed her cheek. "Don't worry about it."

Thankfully, the officers were so busy with the aftermath of the explosions, they didn't notice when I slipped away. I turned on State Road 571, then drove for eight miles before sliding onto a back road. It was the rear entrance to the toxic site, not that anyone ever used it. A mile into Daytona Atomic's property, there was a wooden blockade with large red letters warning of the danger. I eased the car over to the side of the road, got out, moved the barricade, then drove on. After another two miles, I stopped. I opened the trunk and took out the Colt, wrapping the holster around my waist.

I would walk the rest of the way. There was no reason for stealth. I had no doubt the Jackal was equipped with the best technology. He could easily sense a human in the vicinity. He would come out to meet me. He, or it, would be confident in his shielding, but the Jackal wouldn't know about my armor-piercing bullets.

The Florida forest lined the trail for another quarter mile. I walked to the edge of the clearing, seeing piles of trash and debris. It was a lousy place to die.

I took a deep breath, put my hand on the Colt. I reached out and put my left hand on a tough, Florida oak, then looked downward. Things had happened so fast I wasn't sure what to say. Since I had never spoken to God before, I wasn't aware of the divine protocol, if there was one. Lori said God loved all of us humans, with a overwhelming, abundant love. I hoped it was true. I had been pondering all that I've heard Lori say. But sometimes human keep postponing decisions until tomorrow, figuring they have plenty of time. My tomorrow was now.

"If you don't mind a deathbed confession, Lord...I'm betting Lori was right. Lori and Ben. I'd like to join their team. I thought I was unique, I played by my own rules, but now I realize I'm just another, ordinary sinner. Maybe less than ordinary, since I have the blood of Munson Cain on my hands although—" I dropped my tone a half octave—"he wasn't worth a pitcher of warm spit. But I didn't have the right to take his life. Jesus, if you would like my life, what's left of it, please take it. I took one from you, but I'm going to save two."

I didn't know why, but I dropped to my knees.

"Lori rejected me. My own family rejected me. So, Lord, if you're not interested in my offer, it's OK. No one else has been. There's no hard feelings. But heaven or hell, I won't let that thing kill Lori. She's one of your better creations. She, and I'm told, my grandmother." I looked skywards. "Thanks for listening."

I stood up and stared into the site.

The spectre had vanished.

The knowledge straightened my spine. I put my hand on the oak again for support.

The black, hovering spirit was no longer with me. I had been aware of it, off and on, since that day when it predicted my death. But the spectre no longer resonated in my mind or soul. The Grim Reaper's words no longer controlled my destiny.

The thought hit me to turn around. It was almost as physical as a slap in the face. Go back to the house and plunge into holographic fantasies. The house was top security. There was no reason to die on a miserable, contaminated piece of real estate. I could have Lori too. Rather, a fake Lori, and an artificial life. But Helen of Troy seemed real to me. She beckoned to me with a hurricane ferocity. "Come back," she said. I looked toward the toxic waste dump, then turned and glanced east, toward my house.

A choice. Man always has a choice. And like Munson Cain, he can rationalize anything.

Helen motioned to me again. She had launched a thousand ships. But I'd trade a thousand of her for one Lori.

I stepped onto the killing ground.

Twenty-four

It looked like any other dump. If you've seen one dump, you've seen them all. I walked slowly and felt the weight of the gun on my hip. I moved past one pile of debris, turned right and headed down a trail.

I walked between two large garbage piles. Bits and pieces of scrap metal were strewn on the dirt. What looked like a thirty-year-old car fender was off to my right. A collection of equally old tin cans was on my left. I stopped. There was no reason to hunt for it. I'm sure the Jackal had already picked me up on his sensors. I wasn't sure how he could specifically identify Jerico Drake from other humans, but I was confident he could. Long-range retina scans perhaps. Or his sight might be so vivid, he would see me from a mile away and match me with the Drake pictures in his memory.

"Come on out," I yelled. "They didn't program you to hide from me."

For a moment there was only silence. Then I heard a rustling behind one of the scrap heaps, and thought I detected movement behind the six-foot high wall of rusty artifacts.

Then the Jackal walked out slowly, step by step.

He looked a bit like a Guardian. But the deep ugly black color was highlighted by lines of hideous red around the eyes and mouth. His creators were good scientists but clearly had no aesthetic sense. Or perhaps they wanted to give him a horrific look—a soulless creature from the pit of hell. The only other color was the brown of the shoulder holster, with the pale gun stock visable.

He walked out onto the path. Large piles of debris rose up on each side. We stood looking at each other for a minute, like two gunfighters from the old West. I walked toward him. He matched me step by step. We stopped when there was about twenty yards between us. The red lines moved, and I heard the eerie, raspy voice.

"You are Jerico Drake."

"I am. What do they call you?"

"I am the Jackal."

"Not too creative with names, were they?"

He said nothing.

"You've been with me for a long time. Nice to finally see you face-to-face."

If a robot could look puzzled, he would have. "I have never seen you before," he said.

"Met you that day when I was twelve. Never thought I'd get a chance to destroy you." I smiled.

So did he. The hideous lips widened. "I have been ordered to kill you, but not quickly. First, I describe my orders to you, then carry them out."

"I'm always ready for pleasant conversations."

"A bullet for each elbow and for each knee. Then a bullet in the abdomen. Then wait and watch while you die. The execution will be on video and given to Merrill Meeks."

"Do I get royalties?"

No answer.

"What are your other orders?"

"To kill Lori Hallendorf and Ben Adonal. Their deaths do not have to be slow."

"Evil always seeks to kill the righteous, doesn't it?"

Again, he had no answer.

"Their appointments in Samarra have been cancelled."

"I do not understand the Samarra reference, but I have no

cancellations of any orders.

"I plan to cancel them. Neither one of us is walking out of here," I told him.

The red marks widened again into what looked like robotic glee. "You cannot stop me. I am much stronger and quicker than you."

"But I have the strength of ten because my heart is pure."

Silence. He probably didn't get that reference either.

"I suppose there's no reason to drag this out."

He didn't react when I whipped my gun from the holster. A second later he realized his mistake.The *ka-plow* of the colt came a split second before the dull thud as my bullet hit the black chest. With a quickness that startled me, he dove to the ground, but not before a second bullet thudded into his side. The Jackal rolled and pulled his gun. My third shot skimmed an inch over his back. I moved too, but his bullet plunged into the back of my thigh. The impact jarred my hand so my next shots pinged into the sand. His second shot missed, flying over my back. But when I planted my left foot, pain shot through my leg and hip. It slowed me so his third shot grazed my back.

I hit the ground, stretched out on the rugged terrain, and aimed. The Jackal ran toward a wall of metal. He crumpled and sent off red and blue sparks when I blew a knee away. It was a strange sound, not like any bullet explosions I had previously had. It was like hitting mud, a soft plop. He hopped on one black, robotic leg and disappeared behind the debris.

I rolled behind a stand of metal, old car fenders and barrels. I grabbed bullets from my holster and slipped them into the Colt's chamber. My leg was bleeding—not a serious wound, but it did sap my strength. And I couldn't run. The back wound was annoying. Blood trickled down my waist and onto my pants, but I didn't think it was a serious wound either.

"They can't think," Sierra had said. Or maybe this one can think. It sensed immediately I wasn't using regular bullets and started evasive action. My genplus speed allowed me to hit him with a second bullet before he ran. I couldn't sneak up on him, not with his sensors. But he might be crippled too. How quick could he move with most of the right knee blown away? The leg was still attached, but it had to be weakened. I could hear him. He'd make noise when he moved through rusty metal. And how badly did the chest wound hurt him?

I peered out but didn't see anything.

"Bet they told you that you were bulletproof. The best-laid plans of mice and robot scientists..."

"I am damaged," came a hoarse reply. The bullet must have somehow effected his audio panels. His voice wasn't smooth anymore. It sounded labored, and there was an occasional pause between words.

"But I still...function," the Jackal said. "I will....destroy you."

"You got to come get me first, and you aren't walking too well."

"I can repair myself."

Yes, I bet you can, I thought. *I'm sure Merrill's scientists made you self-replicating. Given time, that is.*

"Not when I blow your head off, you can't."

"You can't get to me without me killing you."

"You can't get to me either, you robotic—"

"I don't have to. I am immune to this place, but the radiation will kill you. I just have to wait."

That stunned me. He was right. My skin was already hot and redder than it should be.

"Just have to wait? That's not what Merrill said. He wanted to watch me die. He didn't want a picture after I'm dead. You have to obey your orders."

Actually, Merrill might have preferred slow radiation poisoning to my being gut-shot. But the robot didn't know that. How much flexibility was built in his programming?

I could not sneak up on him, not with his sensors. He could wait me out. I'd slowly die, and he'd slowly repair himself.

I'd have to draw him out.

The trail was six feet wide. On the other side were more barrels, cans, rusted pipes. A robot wouldn't bother to ask why I was moving. But I needed a little bit of luck. I had to hope his shot wouldn't be fatal.

I looked up. "Here's where you come in, Lord."

I gritted my teeth and zig-zagged across the path, my leg pounding with each step. I fired when the Jackal stepped out from his hiding place. I tried to dodge but yelled when his bullet sliced through my chest, spitting out blood and flesh. I spun around and crashed to the sand. My gun flew out of my hand and bounced on the ground.

I waited. The Jackal approached, limping. The dark spectre had waited for more than two decades. He didn't have to rush now. As he edged closer, I bent my right leg back and reached toward the ankle.

The Jackal stood over me and pointed his gun at me.

"Will Merrill mind the extra bullets?"

"One in each elbow and one in each knee, before the abdomen shot."

"That's what I was hoping for...no imagination."

My hand grasped the ankle holster, and I pulled the beretta. It didn't have armor-piercing bullets. The bullets might bounce off the chest, but there were other areas to shoot at.

"Mr. Meeks wanted me to tell you--"

Whatever Meeks wanted to tell me was lost in my rapid fire. The bullets hit their targets. Not soft plops this time. His fingers exploded with a crackling sound. He dropped the gun. Then stared at a robotic hand with two fingers missing and two others dangling by a slender black thread. I groaned with pain but rolled over, kicked his gun away, then drove my good shoulder into his black middle. When we thudded into the ground, pain shredded my arm and chest. He slammed his good arm against me, knocking me off. I frantically looked for a weapon. For the second time, luck—or grace—favored me. I grabbed a handle under a pile of trash, yanked it, and saw it was a baseball bat.

The Jackal had trouble getting up. He'd stand, then the left knee would give way. He had found a lead pipe. It was heavier than the bat, but my weapon was longer. I had a reach advantage.

The red eyes blinked and glowed a deeper color. The red lips moved. "They did not tell me humans were so difficult to kill."

I didn't answer. The chest wound was closer to the heart than I would have liked. I groaned with pain. I didn't have much strength in my left arm.

Hobbling, he approached and swung the pipe. He didn't have my range. I ducked and slammed the bat into his side. He could swivel better than I could. He backhanded me with the pipe, driving me to the ground. I forced the pain down and rose to my knees. Swinging for the fences, I crushed his good knee with the bat. He uttered no sound when he fell to the ground. He tried to rise but the robotic legs wouldn't support him.

On one knee and one hand, I crawled toward my gun. I grabbed it and turned around. The Jackal was on his back, trying to push off the ground with his elbows and crippled legs. I managed two steps toward him. The arm and shoulder protested, but I slowly raised the Colt. After spitting out some blood, I aimed at the dark red eyes.

"Her appointment in Samarra has been cancelled," I told him.

I fired and the right eye exploded. My second shot took out

the left eye. The third sliced away a portion of the black skull. I demolished the rest of his head with my final shots.

I dropped to my knees. Blood spotted the ground from my three wounds. My breathing was labored now. I looked toward the Jackal.

Odd. It was nothing but junk now…useless bits of wires, plastic and whatever else they made robots out of nowadays. But I didn't want to die near it. I didn't know if I would die in a state of grace or whether I'd die on hollowed ground, but I wanted it to be mine, not shared with a creation built by evil men.

I hauled myself across the pathway, groaning with every effort. I left a trail of blood on the sand. After I crawled about twenty yards I turned around. My head hit something soft, so I stayed there, stretched out.

The sun was doing down. Across the tree tops, the sunlight changed into a peaceful, burgundy horizon. A wine, red silence covered the scarred land. The beauty of the horizon reminded me of Lori. She would have a chance now. She'd have a husband, kids, her career, all the simple pleasures and joys of life. As I lost consciousness, I was hoping, in the years to come, she'd think well of me.

I recognized the smile, and the woman. I never realized she had such beautiful brown eyes. She wore a white dress and knelt beside me. Her cool hand touched my face.

"It will be all right, son. I promise."

"It's good to finally meet you, Amelia," I said.

"I've never been far from you, dear. I wished I could have watched you grow up."

I spotted the white cross around her neck. "Glad to see you

picked the right side."

She smiled.

"What was the journey like?" I asked her.

"The destination is wonderful, Jerico."

"Nice to hear."

She touched me again. "It will be all right. I promise."

I awoke with a start. Pain still racked my body, but I smiled. Amelia was correct. It was all right. Lori was safe.

I closed my eyes against the burgundy sun.

Twenty-five

The movement woke me. Irritated, I opened my eyes. A man should be allowed to die in peace. Figures in white radiation suits walked briskly toward me. Two were rolling a stretcher. I watched dispassionately as they moved closer. A shorter, slender figure knelt beside and took off a helmet. I smiled.

"Lori...." The sound was hoarse, little more than a croak.

"Don't talk. Just forgive me, my dear. I almost lost you because of a fool like Munson Cain."

"The hound of heaven," I said.

She smiled. "Yes, but thank your friend Sierra. She heard you shouting at the scientists and told the police you'd be here."

I nodded as best I could.

She took off a thick, white glove and touched my cheek.

"I have a message for you, from my Father and your Father."

"I hope it's good news. I can use some good news."

"It is, my love," she said, as her fingers caressed my cheek. "It's from Isaiah. Chapter 28. 'Your covenant with death has been annulled. Your agreement with the grave will not stand.' "

It took a moment for the words to register. I nodded.

"That's good news," I said.

"It's the best news."

Her fingers swept through my hair and two other white-suited figures lifted me and placed me on the stretcher.

"And I come with the deal," she said. "I've decided I could never find any other man like you."

"Sure you could," I croaked. "I'm only genplus. There are plenty of genrich guys out there."

"Genetics aren't everything. Besides, you'll always be genrich to me."

I grabbed her hand. "Cain. It was accidental. I didn't—" She put a finger to my lips. "I know. I know, honey. It's all right."

"The spectre I wanted to kill, but no human, nothing human."

"I know. I was upset when you told me about Cain, but I realized you couldn't murder any one. Next time, give a girl a chance to change her mind."

I nodded. As they started to roll the stretcher, Lori bent and whispered into my ear. "I want an old-fashioned wedding."

At the hospital I edged in and out of consciousness. It was not an unpleasant experience because, for a while, I heard soft, beautiful songs.

Somewhere, the mermaids were singing for me.

Coming Soon...

A DARK ORANGE FAREWELL

GEORGE L. DUNCAN

Even for veteran detective Jarrold Banyon, this is a baffling case. Two teenagers, whom friends describe as intelligent and stable— and who are new born-again Christians—have fled, allegedly taking two guns and stealing a valuable Aztec idol. Banyon doesn't trust his employers, who seem to care more about the idol than about their runaway daughter.

His search for the modern-day Romeo and Juliet will yield blood, treachery, and death. The key to their disappearance lies decades in the past. Banyon must uncover an ancient secret or a very modern evil will be unleashed on the Earth.

About the Author

George Duncan is a former reporter and now an editorial writer. Although an avid golfer, his game was not nearly good enough to get him on the pro tour, so he became a writer instead. He has sold several stories to Christian e-magazines and has published one previous novel, *A Cold and Distant Memory.* He is now completing his third *novel, A Dark Orange Farewell.* A native of Vero Beach, Florida, he now lives near Harrisonburg, Virginia. He's also a mystery fan. *A Wine Red Silence* sprang from the idea of putting a private detective into the balkanized, politically correct world of the future.

For more information:
www.sffaithgolfer.com
random bits of information about politics, faith, science, science fiction and, of course, golf
www.capstonefiction.com

Printed in the United States
105478LV00002B/9/A